ALL
THE KING'S
MEN

Also by William Mayne

DRIFT

ALL THE KING'S MEN

William Mayne

DELACORTE PRESS ⬥ NEW YORK

Published by
Delacorte Press
The Bantam Doubleday Dell Publishing Group, Inc.
1 Dag Hammarskjold Plaza
New York, New York 10017

This work was first published in Great Britain by
Jonathan Cape Ltd.

Manufactured in the United States of America

First U.S.A. Printing

Library of Congress Cataloging in Publication Data
Mayne, William, 1928–
All the king's men / by William Mayne.
p. cm.
Contents: All the king's men—Boy to island—Stony
Ray.
ISBN 0-385-29626-6
1. Children's stories, English. [1. Short stories.]
I. Title.
PZ7.M4736A1   1988   87-25659
[Fic]—dc19   CIP
                                               AC

For
John and Kathleen Meffen,
Sarah and Elizabeth

CONTENTS

CONTENTS

ALL
THE KING'S
MEN

ALL THE KING'S MEN

1

We were on the way to the winter palace. No one watched us go that year. Fonso kept falling off the dog, and there was no one to see it and laugh, neither as we left the merchanty town nor as we passed along the cold roads between town and forest.

Some villagers gave us a look, and one or two a shout. "Look at the chieftains," said a lad by a fountain, shying a stone at Fonso's dog and hitting it on the flank. The dog yelped and tucked its back legs under, and Fonso fell off again, and clambered up for the thirtieth time, perhaps.

Roberto, up on the horse with me, was out of the basket at once, had the very stone the youth had shied, and flung it back, hard, fast and straight into the still-open laughing mouth. Roberto was at the horse's tail and hauling himself up and into the basket before the youth looked up again after spitting out broken teeth and retching up the stone from his gullet.

Then the dog, between villages, tired of carrying Fonso, and dropped him in the road. Fonso ran after the horse, babbling and calling. He never could make words.

"Joachim," said Hubert to me, "wait for him."

I was the responsible one, the only one with my full senses, so I had the driving of the horse and the finding of the way, and all else to do for the five of us, or seven if you count the animals. I was ready to let Fonso walk further.

He would leap about as much up in the basket with us as he would walking on the road, but he was safe on the road, just falling his own height. If he fell from the horse he might kill himself. He could not knock himself senseless because he was that already.

I slowed the horse, and we waited for Fonso. Hubert was glad of the rest: travelling made him deadly sick, whether by horse or coach. He leaned on the side of the basket, pale and sweating.

Fonso at last realised that we were waiting for him, or he walked into the horse by accident; it was not easy to tell which. He came up by the route Roberto had followed, grasping the horse's tail and walking up a leg. Roberto had come up with dignity, even in his hurry. Fonso came up more like a monkey than a man. But perhaps that was the way with all of us.

All of us. There were five. I am Joachim; I am Swiss, and I am strong, healthy, and sound in my mind and senses, and aged about forty-four years. Hubert is English, aged about twenty-six, and really a good-looking boy. But he is made ill by travel, by the sun, by the cold, by fruit, by flowers, and sometimes all happiness goes from him for weeks and months.

Roberto is our craftsman with hand and eye, to throw a stone, carve wood, fold a doll from a cloth, beat silver into dishes, set a fire for the King, or play the guitar and sing. He is from this country here, and will sometimes go to his home, where they do not want him. In spite of his gifts and skills he is usually working from malice and ill-will, as with throwing that stone, which was more than the youth deserved, because it is right that others should laugh at us in our baskets on the back of a horse, going alone through the villages. Roberto's woodcarving is to make devils or pictures of the King from the wood in the chapel, or, as he did once, make indecent alterations to the statue of Our Lady, so that he was beaten and lodged in jail. But he was soon out again, because some of his other malice is amusing, as when he echoes a singer with his guitar, a shade of tone out of true, a fraction of a beat of time fast or slow, from some distant archway, making the singer fail at the end of a breath, and bringing the King near to tears of laughter (but that was in the old days, and the King at this time was laughing at nothing). He is fifty years old.

Rafe is Italian, but his nation makes no difference to him, since he cannot hear or speak. But his eyes miss nothing, and he speaks with arm and leg and inclinations of the head and shaping of the body. On his best days his aptness and agility and the way he can make any sort of joke will amuse the court for an hour at a time, whatever the business on hand. But again, that has not been possible recently. His age I do not know. He is not young.

Fonso has fallen off the dog enough times for you to know that he is the smallest of us, that he has no pride, that he is young. He is also one of God's children and an idiot, and about fifteen years of age.

We are the King's dwarfs, coming ahead of the court to the winter palace. Most years we are part of the retinue, with the King and the Queen not far behind us, and a troop of soldiers, and music, and then cart after cart of goods for the winter, and dogs and visitors and servants and women. This year we are alone. The Queen died. The King stays this year in the town, where he has need of all his town servants and goods. They say he will come to the winter palace for some hunting at the turn of the year, but no man knows; no dwarf knows.

We have been sent ahead to be out of the way. They say the King is weary of dwarfs, that he only came by us for the Queen's sake, and dwarfs are a woman's plaything. That may be so. The Queen was always well-intentioned towards us, and no unkindness came by her. We are not sure about her daughter, the Infanta. We are glad to be parted from her for a while, even if it is only a week. I am the only one who could ever outface the Infanta, and that now gets more and more difficult for me. The rest of us are unable to manage at all, except by conspiring to keep out of her way. It was not so when her mother lived.

So we went on through the day, five of us in two baskets on either side of a big horse. The dog came back to us and walked alongside. For the most part we stood (because there is no room to sit or squat in the baskets) and said

11

little. Hubert groaned and was sick every so often. Fonso climbed from one basket to another, and Roberto and I caught him each time before he fell, not perhaps for love, since no one loves, or hates, a dwarf; but we are valuable. Roberto pulled twigs out of the weave of the basket and set them round the top lap, plucking at them when he had set them, and played a melancholy tune on them, time after time, until we were wearied by it.

Fonso fell asleep, and we were glad of it. Roberto hoisted the sleeping body up and laid it across the back of the horse between me and Hubert. Roberto and Rafe then set to playing cards with each other over across the horse's rump, the game the French call Brusquembille. They gambled with lead shot stolen from the palace armoury.

The horse trod on its way, feeling nothing of the cardboard weddings and sequences being laid out on its back, knowing nothing of the capture of Aces and tens or the courtship of Queen and Knave in the match called Bezique. Hubert went into a green-faced doze, and something of sleep came to me as well, because when I was aware of the world again there was dusk coming down, and Roberto and Rafe were arguing over a card that could be black or red in the grey light.

The noise woke Fonso, and he began to wriggle his way from the position he was in, hanging face down over the horse's ribs. His struggles took him head first into the basket with Hubert and Rafe, and then all three were wedged in and could not move. Roberto and I were inclined to laugh and leave them to struggle, but the cards fell down to the ground and we had to stop to pick them up. We helped Fonso out and set him to ride on the dog again.

We were nearly at the winter palace. The woodlands we were passing through had made the evening darker than it was, but as we came through the trees we saw the sky ahead of us bright again, and then, high above the river, on its rock, the winter palace, with the sun shining right through it and into our eyes. In three miles we had come to it, up the red rock path and under the archway. Now it was cold, because of the night, and because the winter palace

12

was always cold. The King came here to hunt, not to keep warm. The town palace was warmer in winter, and would have done better for us dwarfs, since we did no hunting. And out here, with forest all round us, we dwarfs were grudged every scrap of firewood by the major-domo, Don Emilio.

Don Emilio cared nothing, in any case, for us dwarfs. The palace gate was locked, and there was no one to attend it. We all climbed from the baskets, except Fonso who had already fallen from his dog out on the path, and banged at the door.

The dog came to us without Fonso, and barked to be admitted. It was more likely to be admitted than we were. "Go fetch Fonso," said Roberto. "Go fetch Fonso, good dog, good boy, fetch Fonso." The dog, of course, started bowing and praying and scampering. "Fetch," said Roberto. "Good boy, bite Fonso on backside."

Fonso came walking in by himself, climbed up on the dog, spurred him to the gate just as it opened, and rode him through. A servant with a lantern let us into his pool of light, among Don Emilio's dogs, who had made a circle round Fonso and our dog, a circle with a waving outside where tails shook and a sharp centre where noses were pointing forwards. Fonso ran his fingers under the risen fur on his dog's back.

Don Emilio did not come to speak to us. A dwarf has privileges direct from the King, but no esteem from the rest of the court. The only person we can speak to as an equal is the monarch; we are below all the rest, from chamberlain to gatekeeper. We are nothing without the King, and now we were sent away from court without him.

There was no food for us. The cook had not heard that we were coming. No one had heard that we were coming. We went down to our place, with the window looking out on the river and the deep colonnade that was nearly our own under the terrace. We thought for a time that a fire had been put there, when we saw red light flickering on a wall, but it was the last of the sunlight coming off the river and fitfully lighting the vault. We were down there alone, cold and tired, and there was no bedding.

Hubert lay on the floor and said he would die. When we had got him up we found he might speak the truth, as he usually does. He was as cold and stiff as a candle, and the same colour when we had him to the edge of the vaults and the light came in a little. Then Rafe touched our backs, to tell us something. He told us he had smelt something, that he had smelt food, and with his gift of mimicry he made us understand that Don Emilio (who was easy to imitate because of his fore-bellied way of walking) and Donna Emilio (who carried her head like a hearth-cricket) were dining above us on the terrace.

So we silently went up the rocks beside the colonnade and over into the terrace and took what we should have been given. Don Emilio came to see us very soon after that, and gave us some more of what we deserved while we licked our fingers. He used a short hard stick that did not sting but raised a bruise. We showed him our backs and let him beat us, and let him shout about our manners and our parentage and our morals, and when he went we had to laugh at Rafe, who followed him out through the vault holding an imaginary stick and lantern to match the real ones of Don Emilio. Only Rafe' could be the man himself, seeming to do nothing different yet making him ridiculous. The way Rafe held his imaginary stick and lantern and moved them about to make shapes we could not see, since there was nothing there to make them, was a marvel, but we dared not laugh aloud. We went to bed on last year's mouldered straw, and we had laughed, though we were bruised and our dinner had not been large: all the pickings from Don Emilio's table would not have filled us, and we had not had all there was (Fonso had giggled and knocked over a jug and we were caught).

The next day we were prisoned to our colonnade and room and not let out. But food was sent down. We sat in the cold sunshine all day, and were glad of peace. Hubert slept. Rafe and Roberto played cards, or Rafe practised new agilities to keep yesterday's travel and bruising from his bones, while Roberto seemed to consider a new song under his breath. Fonso played, and took himself off down to the river. No one would beat him for disobedience, since he could not understand what he was told. I myself brought out the old straw from our room and laid that in the sun and stamped upon the fleas that were livened up by the warmth, because in the night what nourishment we had taken from Don Emilio was taken from us in turn by them with their hungry lips.

That day ended cold again for us. The next was better. We were no longer locked in, and we found we had a new sort of freedom. It is not easy to know what all of us think, because Hubert, for instance, is quiet by nature and does not know much of the language. Fonso says nothing, even less than Rafe. Roberto and I, however, thought we had come on an unexpected holiday and its octave, its following days of peace.

Apart from Don Emilio, who was always to be reckoned with, we were alone with the winter palace servants. No one else from the court was within leagues of us, and we had no duties to attend to, and nothing to do but sit in the sun, eat twice a day, drink five times, and look at every empty apartment in the building.

We had never looked at it all before. Perhaps no one had but Don Emilio and the servants here. We had seen the state apartments and our own quarters, and the church, which was the parish church for the village near by, and that was all. Now we were able to go round the private rooms of the King and the Infanta and the court servants. It seemed to us that we were lodged the worst of all, apart from the others in our cellar-like place, one better than the prisoners and one worse than the dogs.

One day we came back to our room and found a palace workman kneeling there and white-washing the ceiling. The little room is ours because we do not need the height of a full man; the workman thought of the room as a deep cupboard. That night we slept under the colonnade, smelling out there the sweet freshness of the lime on the walls, and pleased that something of our comfort was remembered.

"They will never treat us as men," said Roberto. He was making a song out of the thought, plucking notes from a

15

guitar found in the Infanta's room and letting them fall among the pillars or down to the river. "They will never treat us as children, even, that might one day be men. We are bought and sold."

"They have whitewashed our room, Roberto," I said.

"That is what I say," said Roberto. "They will have washed out the stables first: horses are fit to be sold if they are well kept, and so are we. You will see that we shall be sold, Joachim. You will see."

2

No one gave us a fire in the palace, and we were not let near any made for others. At night we were cold, because it was November. On the third or fourth day of that winter's visit we were at last given a lamp to light us in our quarters at night. But one lamp will not heat five dwarfs; all it will do is give enough light to move about if there is no Fonso to be crawling obscurely underfoot.

We took the lamp out with us, down the rocky bank of the river, not to see by but to give us a flame for a fire. It was no colder out under the sky than it was under the vault of the colonnade. There was stuff to burn down by the water, though some of it was stinking enough, being the rubbish from the palace.

So at night we sat round our fire until the bell rang to show that the gates were to be shut. To get to where we had the fire we had climbed out of our quarters, and had no need of the gate to let us back in, but it was possible for Don Emilio, if he felt like it, to cage in the colonnade, because the palace was a fortified castle and fit for warfare and all its openings could be closed. We knew, because one year we had been locked in, after coming out at night and enjoying some of Don Emilio's wine; after all, though we are despised we are of the King's table, more like his family than his servants, and Don Emilio is only a servant and has his wine as a gift from the King, who is entitled to drink as much of it as he wants, and the same goes for the people of his table. Don Emilio did not listen to our story, but locked us up first, while he barred his wine-store from us in the future, with iron bars.

We had our holiday for a little more than a week, spending our days in the sun and doing nothing. Not even Don Emilio could make us do a hand's turn at anything. For several days he could not manage to keep us out of the state rooms, where we went in and out with the castle servants and the village people who were cleaning and polishing. But when the rooms were clean we were not able to go in there any more. Instead we sat in the sun by the gate and examined all the goods that came in.

"This is the Customs and Examination Patrol," Roberto said to one grocer or butcher or wine-seller after another, as they came, taking samples of their fruit or meat or drink. We were the King's dwarfs, and none of the fellows could say anything to stop us taking what we wanted. Of course, we could not prevent them from telling Don Emilio what had happened to the cheese or oil or cigarros or a certain borrachio of red wine. But Don Emilio did nothing, and we thought we might be safe, Roberto and I (for after all, we were taking nothing more than would make us live as well as if we were in town), at our tricky trade.

We did not know that at the kitchen door there waited Hubert, serious and smart in his black livery, taking the goods in in the name of Don Emilio, and sending Rafe and Fonso up to the house with it, after taking the best that was left. He too thought that we should make our own way in this matter of food.

So we were caught. I think it was some matter of vinegar and eggs that set us out as villains. Don Emilio did nothing in the day, but in the evening, while we roasted our stolen meats at our fire by the water, and were just starting on olives and salt fish and bread, he and the staff of servants came down upon us, pretending not to know us and calling us thieves and brigands and beating us very much, and taking all the food away, half cooked as it was. That is, they took all but the vinegar, and that was our supper. They say vinegar is good against bruising, but we cannot be sure how much worse we would have been without it. It is of little use against hunger.

The next day was Sunday. We went to Mass in the church. The priest, who is one of the King's chaplains and equal to us in some ways, had a clean surplice. By this we knew that the King must be coming during the next week. Also, we thought that the village people had come expecting to see the King, and looked round for him and were disappointed. But they were pleased to see us, because in this part of the country it is lucky to meet a dwarf. In other parts it is a sign of misfortune and not at all lucky. In all parts of the country it is no great pleasure to be a dwarf. So now, in the church, we were simpered at, but not asked any questions, since we are court people and above the villagers.

"Why do they wish to ask us anything?" said Roberto. "Already they know more than we know. They think the King is here, and perhaps he is but we have not been told. We are all like Rafe, it seems, and cannot be told anything, and I am too proud to ask."

I thought that we were humiliated by not being told when our own King was to arrive. Perhaps we were only kept in memory of his Queen, and were more her dwarfs than his, but a Queen is equal to a King, and what either is doing is something we should know before the peasants in the neighbouring countryside.

We heard nothing that day. We thought perhaps the King had come in the night, but in the stables were only Don Emilio's horses and the one that had brought us, and some mules. So the King was not here. But nothing was being made ready, either, and no warming fire was put in any apartment. If there had been one we should somehow have got ourselves to it. As it was we stayed where the sun was and waited.

Rafe and Roberto played their game of cards. Hubert laid a cloth on his head, which is an English custom, and leaned against a wall in the sun. In the town he is never out of doors. Fonso had turned into a dog, we thought, and

19

played in the kennel all day long, and no one hurt him: the dogs have more sense than he has.

The King did not come. Roberto and I were looking all day, but not admitting to each other that we were. Rafe looked as well, and we knew he was looking for the King because he imitated the impatient walk the King has when he paces up and down during tiresome business with boring people.

The next day was Monday. We were woken early by castle servants and brought up to the courtyard. Something had been going on there for some time, because there was still a torch flickering in the cold dawn light. Don Emilio was there, sitting in a chair at a table. We knew what was happening. This was a court of judgement, and criminals were being brought before Don Emilio for judgement and punishment.

"We are to witness a hanging, I dare say," said Roberto. "It is best done before breakfast, I am sure. When the time comes I will cheer the felon on his way with a gallows song."

I could see no gallows, but Roberto did not mind. "Then they will burn him," he said. "There is wood enough." And there was wood enough.

There was no hanging, at last. There were no criminals, but we dwarfs were put up for judgement. Don Emilio brought up the affair of Saturday when we had taken nothing more than our fair share. It was not our fault, only bad luck, that we had taken our fair share twice, but Roberto and I were not going to blame Hubert for having the same idea as ourselves and carrying it out without telling us. We had not told him, because we did not think he would be bold enough to take any part.

We were judged guilty. If we had been men of full stature we could have bought a lawyer to speak for us and the King would have paid. He does not give us coin while we stay in his service, but pays us when we leave or die. So now he would have paid a lawyer and taken it from our pensions or departure money.

Our sentence was that from this moment on, until Don Emilio returned from the journey he was about to start on now (which he had risen early to begin the sooner), we were all five to be lodged in the stocks outside the palace gate. It was a punishment for us, a warning for all, and it showed all who came on business that if they saw us again it was as criminals and not as a Customs and Examination Patrol.

So there we were lodged, without food and drink, all five, and men came to see from miles around. There was no pity for any of us, but few stones were thrown. Our hands were free, and when the first stone came Roberto kept it. At the throwing of the second one he sent back the one he had before, flinging it smoothly so that it hit above the man's ear and went whirring off into a ditch. The man was helped away bleeding. After that we were left alone, because all the peasants who lived near had seen us and were no more interested.

By the middle of the day, when we were left alone, we had the stocks broken and pulled apart. Dwarfs are very strong. We had the wood ready to replace across our legs when anyone came. We should not have let Fonso out, because he would not stay with us but had to run off to the kitchens and find some food. He did not go short any more than a dog does.

We stayed by our stocks, ready to lock ourselves in when Don Emilio came back. We had to remain hungry, and that was now our worst burden. Don Emilio returned at about four o'clock, riding ahead of one of the King's coaches. We were in place before he arrived, but he took no notice of us at all, and had forgotten us. He rode straight past and went into the palace. We heard him walking up the steps with his spurs grating on the stone.

The coach seemed empty. "Don Emilio has done away with the King," said Roberto, making up a story to account for it. "He has gone into the palace to proclaim his wife Queen. They will ride to town in that coach, but I think a wheel will come off his ambition."

The coach went into the yard and out of our sight. I said that since Don Emilio had returned we should loose ourselves from the stocks, so that we could see what was happening in the yard, whether Don Emilio was indeed

21

about to set out again. If he did there would be bad reasons for it, and bad times for dwarfs.

Roberto and I thought we had better stay as we were for a little longer. Then a stone came skidding down the castle wall at us, thrown by some invisible hand. Roberto had one of his own all ready, balanced and polished and ready to split a skull. He was looking for the skull when Rafe and I each put an arm in front of him.

The stone that had come down the castle wall had been thrown by the Infanta, and of course it would not hit us, since she is only a little girl of six. She had climbed on the wall and thrown a stone, and now she came running out of the castle gate calling to us by name, "Roberto, Rafe, Joachim, Hubert," and throwing more stones.

We were glad to see her, though we had been thankful to be away from her a week before. She did not treat us with any sort of kindness, and had not been brought up to. She knew we were neither proper people nor animals and were no use, except that we might be sold to another house if we were no longer wanted, and she treated us most of the time like dolls she hated.

But we were glad to see her hurtling from the gateway, scattering stones, running dizzily, and shouting. She had been travelling all day and like Hubert she was bad at it, and she was pale and ill-looking, and had to stop running to be sick in the road.

"I fear she is happy," said Roberto. "Our rest is over."

She was happy, but only because she had been bored and ill for the journey. Her lady-in-waiting came after her, calling for her but not being able to catch her up. The lady-in-waiting was wearing town shoes and her ankles began to turn. The Infanta's shoes were not much better for walking in the country road, and she tore them off and threw one at Rafe and one at the lady-in-waiting. Then she was caught, because she could not bear the weight of her feet on the stones.

The lady-in-waiting took her back to the gateway, pulling one shoe on to her, and taking the other from Rafe and putting that on too. We had all come from the stocks and stood round watching, waiting to be spoken to again.

22

The Infanta watched her feet being put into shoes, miscalled the lady-in-waiting, and was gently sick again in the road.

The lady-in-waiting looked at us but did not find the right words to say. She despised us, of course. She dragged the Infanta towards the castle ready for the stupid little ceremony of being given the key from Don Emilio. The King thought this piece of make-believe was a bore, and would walk up and down while the talking was going on. The Infanta was not going to listen at all, and walked straight past Don Emilio, who stood there with the key that fitted no door (Roberto and I had tried it two years before and told the King, who had laughed). Donna Emilio tried to stop the child and return to her duty by picking her up and bringing her to Don Emilio. The Infanta was furious at that and began to scratch and bite and scream. The ceremony was abandoned. The key was put on a wall and Don Emilio went to see to his wife, who dropped the Infanta. The Infanta lay on her back and kicked the ground, raising dust, and went on screaming. Donna Emilio, dabbing blood from her cheeks with a handkerchief, stood by her. Don Emilio, looking as if he would call another court and have the Infanta flogged, his own hand twitching to do it, stood uneasily beside his wifc. The lady-in-waiting stood coldly the other side of the Infanta and waited, doing nothing.

"Ha-oomph," said Don Emilio after a time, and he turned and went into the palace.

"Ha-oomph," said Roberto, in exactly the same tone, loud enough for Don Emilio to hear.

The Infanta stopped screaming, sat up, and laughed at Roberto, and snivelled as well, because her nose was full of tears.

"See what you have done," said the lady-in-waiting, turning the Infanta's wet head towards Donna Emilio and her scratched face.

The Infanta put out her tongue and blew a certain sort of noise at Donna Emilio. Don Emilio came back from the palace door and took his wife's arm in his left hand. With his right he wielded his riding crop to hit Roberto across

23

the face if he could, somehow trying to match Donna Emilio's wounds. We all stood back and watched the lady-in-waiting taking the Infanta indoors, and Don Emilio following ten yards behind.

As she went the Infanta continued making the noise. And every few paces she hitched up her skirt and wriggled her bare backside towards Donna Emilio, to show her what she thought of her. Don Emilio's riding switch tugged at his hand.

"I wish he would," said Roberto, under his voice.

"Her ladyship is back," said Hubert, in his gentle, resigned English way.

I said nothing. But our short holiday was over. No one said anything about the stocks, where we should have been.

24

3

We took the abandoned key from where Don Emilio had left it on a wall. "We can be of service to the King with it, when he comes," said Roberto. "I do not know how."

But Rafe, unable to hear or say, smiled and clapped his hands and knew what he would do. He would not show us at the moment, in case Don Emilio watched from a window and understood. All we did at the time was to look in the coach the Infanta had come in, to see whether there was anything to eat.

We found some dainty biscuits and some sweetened brandy well let down with water, and we shared those as we went. There was nothing else to eat. There was the baggage of the lady-in-waiting, and the little hampers of the Infanta, but we left those, because we are not servants to fetch and carry. There was a wooden doll, and a cloth doll, lying on the seat. We thought we might do ourselves a good turn by taking them up to the Infanta, and cast lots about who should go, drawing cards to see the highest. Roberto drew a King, and was ready with the dolls in his hands before I drew my card, which was a ten. In Brusquembille the ten is higher than the King, so I had won, if that was the game we measured by.

Roberto and I began to argue about it, shouting at each other, because neither of us wanted to go, yet we both thought someone should. Then we found we were both shouting the same thing, which was "Send Fonso and the dog," and neither of us meant it. Fonso and the dog would never get there. But Roberto and I could blame each other if the dolls were lost for ever, and we would have accidentally done the Infanta a bad turn.

Hubert stopped us. "Draw once more," he said. "All of us. Decide what order the cards are judged in, and abide by that."

We decided on the Brusquembille order, Ace, ten, King, Queen, Knave, nine, eight, seven, and drew again. This time Hubert had a ten, Rafe had a seven, Roberto had a Queen of Spades, and I had the Knave of Diamonds. So we had a problem again, because in Brusquembille the seven is sometimes as valuable as the ten or the Ace, and we were not sure of their order. But Roberto and I had between us the pair called Bezique, and together they were worth more than the others. So Roberto and I went up with the dolls.

The higher we went in the castle the darker it was as the walls closed in on us, until we were high enough to come up to the sun once more. It had left the courtyard below (where we could see Hubert and Rafe impeding the palace servants who wanted to take the coach away) in shadow, but glowed still on the far mountains. It shone through one of the western windows, coming through the river valley to do so, as it did down in our colonnade and on the terraces. Up here, in the throne room, a double window cast a double light on the two thrones, one for King, one for Queen, standing against the back wall, one of them empty for the time being until the King came, the other empty for the best part of a year already, since the Queen died.

"I, myself, would take one of those away," said Roberto. "There can be no joy to King or Infanta in it. And," he added, hoisting himself into the Queen's throne, "there is no great comfort in it, if she were here, may her soul rest in peace."

We were a moment only at the Infanta's apartment. Here the sun was locked out, and the cold. Lamps flared in

26

the room, a fire leapt in the hearth. On a bearskin by it sat the Infanta with her hair braided, plaguing one of the palace kittens. There was smell of spice and a gentle odour of soup, scent of fresh linen under a flat-iron.

"Oh yes," said the lady-in-waiting, "one had been wondering where the dollies were, hadn't one, your highness?" The Infanta leapt up from her place and bustled across the room in a great spreading nightgown, clutching the kitten and her bowl of soup in one hand and holding the other out for the dolls. The lady-in-waiting took the dolls from us, shook them, and handed them over to the grasping hand.

"One wishes to thank you," she said. "Monsieur, er ..." She always seemed to forget our names unless she wanted to blame us for something, and then she had the right one quick enough.

"Monsieur Bezique," said Roberto. "As one can see." We bowed. She looked coldly at us. The Infanta scurried back to the fire, being clawed by the kitten. One closed the door, still giving us one's cold look.

The next day there were more arrivals. The first to come were carts loaded with household stuffs. We all sat on a wall in the sunshine and watched the arrivals, doing nothing to help, of course. Every time Don Emilio appeared in the courtyard, which was often, we jumped down from the wall, ran under his feet as much as we could, and arranged ourselves in the broken stocks, which was to mock him and his punishment.

We had always assumed that the palace was furnished throughout, ready for any number of guests. It was furnished plainly, in much the style it was built in, because it was a castle in the first place, not a palace, and the King came here in winter not for warmth (as we knew) but for the sake of the hunting. There were wolves and wild boar and deer and bear in the forests and on the mountains, and within the castle across the season were men the match and manner of all these beasts. There was nothing dainty about winter visitors, and there was nothing dainty in the appointments of the castle.

The furniture being brought in now was different, new

27

and soft and bright. There were carpets for floors, for instance, and perhaps the Infanta would sit no more on the bearskin slain by some wild baron who hung, as I have seen, his sword in the curtains and lodged his spear with its point bloody in the very table he was eating from.

"Softer living for the King will mean softer living for us," said Roberto. "I shall be glad."

We were outside all day, and did not see where the furniture went, or how anything was disposed. I remember that when we went in as the sunlight died Don Emilio was complaining towards his kitchen that the terrace where he and Donna Emilio were dining was full of smoke, and he then had to turn to the Infanta's lady-in-waiting who had come down the great stair and begun to tell him that there was smoke in their apartments, and that one could not see across one's cot.

We went down to our place. There was nothing of our doing in what they were talking about.

Yet it was concerned with us. No one had told us, and we had not in the least expected, that our colonnade was set with tables and chairs and lengths of mat, like an apartment higher in the castle. All was open to the weather still at the river end, and was full of dusty smoke coming in from the river bank. But there was a clean fire in our fireplace, and logs beside it. And in the bedroom were beds, two of them only, it was true, but beds to replace the boards and straw. It was that straw that seemed to have been turned out of the end of the colonnade and set on fire on the bank below that caused the smoke there was complaint of. More amazing than the fact that someone had thought of us at all was the fact that they had thought sensibly. All the chairs and tables and beds were of a size that we would be comfortable at; not much smaller than a full man's table or chair, but a little less, for after all a child can manage pretty well at an ordinary table.

The straw outside burnt away. The smoke cleared. Our fire burnt cheerfully. Hubert went up and stole some beer from the kitchen, and warmed it English fashion at the fire, and we drank it and were content.

28

The beds were a tight fit, but it was for a night only, we were sure, and more would come the next day, or be in the cart in the yard now, waiting to be unloaded.

The Infanta was briskly about in the morning. First she went for a stylish walk with the lady-in-waiting, and then she came down to the yard alone, like any child. She had come to play and worry us, or a kitten, or some other constrained and helpless creature. We kept a little out of her way at first, until it was more trouble to do that than to submit to being played with.

She was not too much trouble at first. There was a wheelbarrow in the yard, and with four of us strong and sensible enough to give her rides she was happy for a long time, and it was little trouble to us.

Then, of course (but it is not our place to tell her), she felt sickly from being taken about, and blamed us, and sat among us moaning and moving her jaws and running with dribble at the mouth until she felt better.

Hubert had found, in his little bundle of household goods that he carried everywhere, a piece of felt. Somewhere else he had found a feather. From them he had made himself a hat to sit in the sun with, better than the kerchief he had used before. He was wearing the hat now, and the whole castle had seen it and remarked on it, because there was something English and insolent about it, tipped over one eye and the feather raking upwards, and intended, in good time, to get up Don Emilio's nose, which was something we talked about loudly when he could hear. So the hat was well known.

The Infanta took it from his head and ran away shrieking, into the palace under the feet of the servants moving furniture. The servants stood aside to let her through, but made a great stickle with their legs when we wanted to pass and delayed us a little. We were all part of the Infanta's game, so it was fair. But we lost her, hearing her shoes clatter off into the passages and interconnecting rooms, and not knowing where to go after her.

We looked about for a time, but no clue came. The Infanta had probably tired of the game and dropped the hat somewhere, and would not know where, because she is

29

only six years old. We were grown men in our years, though we were no bigger than the Infanta. We too could tire of a game, and we tired of this one. We went back to the yard, through the palace.

There was no sign of the Infanta, but after all she was not our responsibility. But we had to wonder, because she is the King's daughter and we are of his table and in some ways equal.

We did not find her. We found an outcry instead, with Don Emilio waiting in a doorway for us, holding Hubert's hat.

I do not know what the Infanta had done. I believe she had overset a barrel of pickles in the store-rooms, but we were blamed, and most of all Hubert, and we were all beaten. I wondered whether the Infanta might be herself floating in vinegar somewhere, but since there was no cry from the lady-in-waiting then she could not be lost.

We were well beaten by the time Don Emilio had done, but we were not put in the stocks again. We were deprived of a meal, too, as if we had had our fill of pickled cucumber or onion or eggs. We wished for the King to come, and then we should have a friend at Court.

We stayed indoors the rest of the day, down by our fire. We talked, and played Brusquembille, slept, and were idle. We heard the Infanta's voice raised in protest far above us once, and the lady-in-waiting working hard to keep her temper.

Towards the end of the day we heard Don Emilio shouting too, on the terrace above, with Donna Emilio helping him with worried mutterings. Don Emilio was looking for the key.

"Ha," said Roberto. "He does not have it. But the King is coming, and will be here at any moment, or Don Emilio would not look for the key." He made signs to Rafe, who remembered what he had decided to do with the key when the King came, to mock Don Emilio. Roberto gave him the key and we went up into the yard.

The King was not here yet. The yard was still empty, but for one horse that had come on ahead with a messenger or equerry, and a small pony trap that would have nothing to do with the King and belonged to some merchant selling supplies to Don Emilio.

There were people waiting for the King to appear. We waited with them for a time until we realized that most of them were kitchen workers and that the kitchen would be empty. It was, but all we took was bread and cold meat, no more than we had missed, and one leather bottle of wine.

"We shall complain better to the King about our hunger if we sharpen our wits by eating first," said Roberto.

When we came out again it was because we heard the wheels of a coach in the yard. Nearly everybody now had gathered to watch Don Emilio's welcome.

Robert nudged Rafe. Rafe understood well enough. But we did not run forward at that time, because Don Emilio was not quite ready. He was still having keys brought to him, hoping to find a suitable one.

No one had yet alighted from the coach. If he had much work the King travelled in one of the royal diligences, and perhaps now, even though he had reached his destination, he was busy in the middle of a letter.

Then, at a word from inside, a footman came to open the door, and that was our signal. We knew the King was in the coach and would not come riding up behind it, having travelled by horse.

The Infanta went tripping across the yard ahead of us, and we followed, not minding about her but wanting to be under Don Emilio's feet, and to mimic his ponderous way of giving the King a useless key.

We caught up with the Infanta, Roberto and Hubert on either side of her. And just there, standing where it had been left that morning, was the wheelbarrow. We knew what to do. I lifted the handles of the barrow, Roberto and Hubert took the Infanta's arms and hoisted her up, I ran the barrow underneath, and she sat in it and we went off at a run towards the coach.

Then, several things were wrong. Because I saw, standing among the people, next to the lady-in-waiting, the Infanta. It was not the Infanta in the barrow, but some other child. Roberto and Hubert, steadying our passenger,

31

found that something was wrong too, and the passenger herself was not pleased and began to shriek.

The coach door was open now. From it there stepped not the King, but a lady whose picture we had seen, who was known to us. She was Mathilde, the red-headed Queen of Burgundy. She stood and looked at our noisy unruly riot. We stood and looked back. From the wheelbarrow there climbed with great dignity a sallow and angry full-grown lady dwarf obviously belonging to the Queen. Before going forward to her mistress she turned and slapped first Roberto's face and then Hubert's.

There was silence in the yard. Rafe felt it was so, and put away the key. Fonso came bubbling up and jumped into the barrow with his dog. That was how we welcomed the Burgundian Queen.

4

Don Emilio gave the Burgundian Queen a key. We would
have mocked him if we could, but we had our own
troubles to deal with. We had gone forward to give a
friendly and humorous greeting to our own King, and
instead we had insulted one of his guests and affronted her
servant or lady-in-waiting, and we had been left where
everybody could see us and had to take ourselves away in
some proper manner.

It was difficult, with the idiot Fonso and his dog in our
wheelbarrow. The Burgundian Queen Mathilde was looking at us with distaste. Her dwarf woman had gone up to
her and curtsied and stood beside her, swallowing angrily
and with her face twitching, and looking at us with hatred.
Don Emilio, with his replacement key, was coming across
the courtyard. Roberto and I took a handle of the barrow
each, Fonso waved, the dog stood up, sat down, put a paw
on the side of the barrow and upset the lot. Roberto and I
went down with it. Fonso picked himself up and started to
climb on the dog. The dog was bored with that, and shook
him off, knocked him down, took hold of his shirt and
carried him away. Fonso giggled.

The rest of us did the best we could. Roberto thought
fastest for us, in this case, though perhaps Rafe was
quicker. But Rafe could not tell us quickly what to do.

33

Roberto pushed Rafe into the barrow and sat him down. Then he told me and Hubert to push it by the handles, and while we did that he pushed at the wheel, against us. Then he made us pull, and we stood there struggling and unable to move the wheel at all.

Don Emilio made an angry gesture to us to go away, but we were stuck. He had to come across himself, sweeping the air with his hand to show us we had to go. Rafe imitated him, and even had the key in his other hand, like Don Emilio.

Before we were in danger of being struck we picked up the barrow and ran off with it. As the barrow went up in the air Rafe leapt out high, somersaulted over our heads, whirled his way, still somersaulting but curled up, through Don Emilio's legs, and followed us out.

"The crowd was for us," said Hubert, when we were at the back of the yard again and were safe.

"I do not care about the crowd," said Roberto. "I am the King's dwarf."

"We went to meet the King," I said. "We are of the King's table. Don Emilio should tell us what is to happen. We may not wish to meet the Burgundian Queen."

"We did not wish to meet her lady attendant," said Hubert, rubbing his cheek.

"We have had worse cuffings from the Infanta," said Roberto. "Many a time."

"Maybe," said Hubert. "Harder perhaps; but this lady was skilful."

We watched the Burgundian Queen into her lodgings, and saw the lights go up inside the windows as the sun went down. Until now the palace had been dark at night, and that had made us feel homeless; all the dark hollow stone above had drawn our town-living spirits into its own blackness. The Infanta's small apartment had shown two small windows, no more. Don Emilio's windows looked only on to his own courtyard, and we never saw them. But now there was some life in the towers, even if it only came from a hunting guest.

Our supper was given to us in a basket by one of the kitchen girls. There was to be no table for the court that

34

night, no place for us. We ate and drank on the bailey wall, where the kitchen chimney came up it, and watched the lights across in the bigger building, and then threw the basket down to the kitchen door and went to our lodgings, taking the wine to drink round our own fire.

The King could not be far behind his guests, we thought. Perhaps tomorrow we should have our rights of equality restored, our proper dignity given back to us. We thought of going to ask Don Emilio when the King would come, but we were too proud. All we took from him at that time was a candle to give us flame when we lit our fire down in the vault.

The fire was already lit, candles were already glowing, when we opened the door. We were beginning to feel appreciated, and were on the edge of forgiving Don Emilio (to some extent and for a limited time) for his behaviour towards us, when we saw we were not the first here tonight, were not the only ones using the room.

Walking elegantly back from the far end, where he had been looking out over the river, was a slim black dwarf, smoking a cigarro and looking at us in a puzzled and superior way.

"Who are *you*?" he said. "We've everything we need tonight; you can run along now."

"Who is it, Bouk old boy?" said another voice, and from the same far end of the room came another smartly-dressed dwarf, with a red face and a head like a Dutchman.

"Nobody we know, Piet old man," said the black dwarf.

The one called Piet looked at us, with our untidy commonplace clothes, our leather bottle of rough wine, and our stolen candle. "Egad," he said, full of scorn. "Is there anything you want, you fellows?"

So we understood then that all the suitable furniture we had found, the tables and chairs and beds, had not been for us at all but for these two dandies; that the firewood and candles had not been for our comfort and use; that we had been turned out of our accustomed place when we had thought it was getting better for us, and we had been told nothing about it.

I felt Roberto beside me beginning to tremble with rage.

35

I feared that at any moment he would do something violent and hurl a chair at the black man, who stood looking at us like a Duke, or the Dutchman, who looked at us as if we were dogs of doubtful quality.

"Don't," I said to Roberto.

"Keep calm," said Hubert, stepping past us on the steps. He lifted his cheeky hat and put it on his head again. "Evening one and all," he said, and walked across to the fireplace and sat down. "Bring on the wine," he said, picking up a glass the two dandies had been using and throwing its contents into the back of the fire. The glass had held brandy, and there was a gush of smoky flame. "Hey up," said Hubert, lifting off his hat and stroking the feather. "Mind my tailpiece."

We walked across to him and sat on chairs or the floor or, like Fonso, on the dog. There was another glass. Rafe hurled its brandy into the back of the fire, and there was another gush of flame. Fonso began to burn gently, but we smothered the flames. Fonso rested his head on the dog, lay on the floor, and warmed his bottom. The rest of us shared the two glasses and the leather bottle of wine.

We did not get much of it. Master Bouk, the black one, came across and drew a little rapier. "You fellows had better go away, don't you know," he said.

Roberto smacked his lips and refilled the glass. Bouk swung the rapier and necked the glass. The foot and stem stayed on the table, but the bowl tipped off complete, rolled over spilling its red contents, and dropped to the floor, breaking to wet splinters.

"Cheers," said Roberto, and he lifted the bottle to his lips. The little rapier flashed up towards the bottle and cut an invisible gash in it once. There was a small flow of dampness from this first wound. The next one (and all the time Roberto's throat swallowed unhurriedly) joined it, and there was a little flow of wine. The third cut joined both the others and a triangle from the leather was cut out.

Roberto took no notice of what was happening. We were bound to ignore the intruders who had stolen our room. Roberto drank on, but the wine poured to the floor far faster, and soon he sucked air only. He lifted the bottle down, sighed, wiped his mouth, smiled, belched, examined the bottle to see that it was truly empty, and then slapped Bouk across the side of his face with it, knocking him down on top of Fonso and the dog, so that all three of them were struggling on the floor out of the way.

Roberto did a truly wicked thing next. He picked up the dropped rapier and thrust it into the fire, where the heat would soften the metal and make it useless and dangerous. Rafe pulled it out at once, and Roberto did not notice, since he was now attacking Piet.

The fight was three to three. Fonso did not count. He thought that Bouk was trying to tickle him, and there were joyful shrieks and barks underfoot. Hubert and I went to the rescue of Piet, who was parrying the leather bottle with his small sword, but not hurting Roberto. We took hold of Roberto and strapped his hands with the strap of the bottle and sat him against a table. I took the rapier from Rafe and kept peace between Roberto and the black dwarf, who was free of Fonso now. Hubert and Piet were fighting a mock battle, one with the small sword, the other with the feather from his hat.

"We shall see what comes of this," said Bouk in a little while. "Leave these oafs alone, Piet, and come with me." And the pair of them went off up the stairs, though not before Piet, with a little flick of the wrist, lopped the end off Hubert's feather.

We loosed Roberto from the table leg. He was still full of anger, but he could still see clearly what would happen next. We should be punished by Don Emilio. That was nothing new any winter, because he had us in his power, and, though we always said we had the ear of the King, we did not always make him care.

We were punished. Don Emilio came himself, bringing four of the heavier servants. We were thrown out of our own quarters, beaten with sticks, cursed, abused, kicked, and given one of the rooms in the bailey wall next to the kennels, with no window but the doorway, nor door but a horse-skin a hundred years old, and the place so low that even we had to lie down to be in it at all. We could of course see all that went on in the courtyard, and so could

37

all in the courtyard see all that we did, except at night, as it was now, when even we could not see how we were lodged, only smell it.

Bruises did not show much on the black dwarf, but we thought his face was swollen. Piet had a black eye and a cut lip. Their clothes had been made worse by the fight, but the next morning they had another set each. They came out into the courtyard and took no notice of us.

The Burgundian Queen's woman dwarf came out the Queen's lodgings and across to the kitchen with some message.

"I shall not make that mistake again," said Roberto.

"But you have had worse from the Infanta," said Hubert.

"It is different," said Roberto.

The Infanta and the Burgundian Queen met at about mid-day, in the middle hall of the palace, with the wintry sun stooping in through the high windows and laying folded squares of light part on the floor and part on the wall, now and then lighting the head of some passing person. The Burgundian Queen stood with her head in a ray of light, and her shadow on the wall was ringed with gold circles of sun, and the picture was living with movement and rising waves.

The Infanta was the one graciously giving audience to the Queen, but there was a score of years between them, and one was only a Princess, after all, and the other a crowned Queen with a kingdom. We were there, as well as we could be, smelling of the kennel, as the only courtiers the Infanta had.

We had trouble keeping her on her chair before the Queen came, because she wanted to have horse rides and to be swung. The lady-in-waiting did what she could to keep her still.

The Queen came and stood there shining. The Infanta blinked at her, because she was very bright in that gloomy room. "I can stand on my head," said the Infanta, jumping from the chair and running to the wall, and over the sunlight and shadow of the Queen kicking up her heels and putting them on the wall. The lady-in-waiting ran across to her and lifted her skirts up to what was respectable. "Hold me, hold me," said the Infanta, upside down, and red in the face.

The Queen gave her the cold look. From close against her skirt, where we had not seen her, the dwarf woman appeared, and followed her majesty out. The Infanta's lady-in-waiting then sat on the Infanta's chair and embroidered, while we and the dog played at a number of games with the child, which is our duty. She is now bigger than Roberto and bigger than me, and for a long time has been bigger than Hubert or Rafe and of course Fonso. But I think the dog is heavier. Somehow, when the Infanta was smaller we dwarfs were more equal with the lady-in-waiting. Now that we are all about the same size the lady-in-waiting has grown more remote from us.

It was as well that we lived now in the wall. The King came that night on horseback very late. He had sent a rider on ahead to warn Don Emilio, but no one told us, of course. We first knew when lights were brought into the courtyard. We went to sit under one of the torches to play cards. Then the Infanta came across the cobbles, limping barefoot in her nightgown, with the lady-in-waiting hobbling in her high heels after her. The Infanta made for the gate calling for Daddy, and he appeared, closing his eyes against the glare inside.

The Infanta fell over. We hastily dropped the cards and assembled yesterday's trick with the wheelbarrow, and this time it was the Infanta we picked up. I do not think it was our fault, in the dark, that we did not notice how the barrow had been used for cleaning out the stables not long before. But the Infanta did not mind, no more did the King, and we brought them together, and were in front of Don Emilio with his silly ceremony of the key, and had one in the King's hand before the Don was halfway across the yard.??Äjust near enough to see what was happening.

The King took up his daughter and set her in front of him on the horse.

"Sire," said Roberto, "we welcome you heartily. We have many grievous complaints for your ear, Sire."

"Tomorrow, Roberto," said the King. "Is the lady-in-waiting here?"

"Sire," said Roberto, and he took the Infanta down from the horse and gave her to the lady-in-waiting, who smelt the horse dung on her and looked at us with displeasure.

"The Burgundian Queen, is she here?" said the King, when Don Emilio came to him. "Send to her and say I have come. Here, Hubert, take my horse." And the King went off at once towards the Queen's lodging.

5

The King knocked at the Queen's door with his own hand.
All of us would have saved him the trouble if he had
spoken. But he walked past us, and we were all grinning
with delight to see him; he walked past the lady-in-
waiting and the Infanta; he walked past Don Emilio and
the spurious key, and ignored Donna Emilio. Since he had
come to the palace alone there was no one else he could
ignore.

Don Emilio turned about and hesitated, rattling the key.
He would no doubt have started to blame us for our trick if
the King had not been there; but of course if the King had
not been there there would have been no trick.

The King waited outside the Queen's door. There was
darkness at the foot of the wall where he stood, and the
windows immediately above were dark too. The higher
ones were still lit, however. The light from them came
gradually down the stonework, showing from the narrow
slits of the servants' stair as each twist of the spiral
brought the travelling lamp lower.

Then there was a lit archway, because the door had
opened. In the doorway stood the Queen's dwarf woman,
with the light behind her. The King stood outside, and he
stayed outside. The dwarf woman did not let him in. She
closed the door and we heard the bolts drop. We saw the

41

light ascend the spiral stair opening by opening, leaving darkness behind it again.

The King stood a moment, then turned to his own door in the further tower, opened it on to darkness, and went in into darkness, unattended.

Don Emilio had gone in to his illuminated home. No one else was here to go with the King. Hubert had come back from taking the King's horse to the stable and was busy fastening a black plume from some horse decoration to his hat, where Piet's small sword had cut off the first feather he had.

"Lights for the King," I said, but there was no one to hear but four out of us five, and no one to understand but three of us. We went into the kitchen and took candles and followed the King into his apartments.

The King was very quiet. He was not below, but he would not be. He was not in any apartment of state, where they stood in the night cold and clean and empty. He was not in the private room where there should have been an evening fire for him. He was not in the dining-room, where there should have been a supper for him. We lit his evening fire, and we lit the lamps on the walls.

We found the King. He was on his bed, asleep in his riding clothes, hat and boots and spurs and a great gauntlet on one hand, the other gauntlet lying beside him like a crab.

Hubert and Roberto began to giggle a little. They said that the King looked like me, Joachim, "when you were drunk last Christmas," Hubert said.

"Why that?" I asked, because the comparison seemed not in favour of the King, and therefore unmannerly.

"Because it was necessary to remove your boots," said Hubert, "and there was danger in that. You might have kicked us, Joachim; the King might have us hanged for touching him."

We took him off his boots. He woke and called us his good little fellows, and slept again. We laid a cover on him, and went to sit by the fire in the sitting-room, where there was light and warmth. Hubert went downstairs and out and across to our kennel and brought the pack of cards, and we lay on the sewn deerskins playing Brusquembille and sleeping and hungering.

We were not left long. There was noise of more arrivals in the courtyard. We looked out, but there was little to see but a lantern moving about, from here just showing itself, and now and then a face or a hand. It was the King's own servants arriving. The King had stayed with them most of the day, but at the end had ridden on ahead to have speech with the Burgundian Queen, but had had a wasted journey. The King's servants were no enemies to us, and we were none to them. We were pleased that they had remembered to bring our Court clothes, even if the cloth was thin for winter. The boxes were in a following cart, they said. Then we left them with the King, because they had two days' work in an hour. Never before, they said, had they come anywhere after the King but always two days before. It was no fault of theirs, and no ordinary man could blame them for it; but kings, even our own King, think their own thoughts. There is no one in the land greater than the King, I thought. But I was in some way wrong, as it will appear.

In the next days we were very much irked by the sight of the Queen's dwarfs, the two men, strolling about in their dainty clothes, eating fine meats and white bread, and drinking all manner of liquors that our stomachs thirsted for. Roberto said he did not know which was the worse sin, envy or drunkenness, and there was no one to ask, because the question would be thought frivolous by the priest, who ought to be able to tell us.

We had words once or twice with the little black man and his Dutch companion, but they offered us nothing, only standing aside to avoid all possibility of being touched by us (we had been thanked by the King for taking off his boots, remember, and who is a higher power than that?), and making lofty remarks to one another about peasants and serfs and slaves.

We were happy to see the Infanta, one day, catch the black man and be fascinated by him. When he was in royal hands he could not struggle or draw his sword or protest. He had to submit to one of the child's playtimes, and came out of it very much ruffled and wet with being washed, and hurt again from having his head touched where the empty wine bottle had hit it. We were glad to see him helpless, and hoped the little Dutchman might be treated next; but at the same time we were jealous that our own Infanta was interested in any other dwarf. We are the King's dwarfs, and she is the King's child.

We tried to speak with the King. We were sure he did not know that we were turned out of our usual place and made to live with the dogs. The servants told us they had spoken with the King, because servants are able to do so. The King said that we should meet as time went on, and of course we did, but being in the same room for a time in the day is not the same as audience and time to speak your troubles.

The King went hunting three days that week. The first time he went with Don Emilio, to see what game there was this year. There was a time when I went on the hunt too, but I have aged faster than the King. Roberto hunts with a stone in either hand and knocks down flying birds. Hubert claims a skill of being able to set snares on a moonlit night, and sings an English song to prove it, but has never done it to prove it.

Only Fonso would go hunting, riding and tumbling among the hounds, and being left on his own a mile from the palace and waiting for the hunt to come back to him. Sometimes he has been scented by the hounds, hunted down, and worried by their tongues. One day he will be torn up and his face hung on the palace wall with a date below it and the place, and he will continue, probably, to dribble on visitors. Rafe would watch the hunt away and be thoughtful and unable to express anything of what he felt.

There were three of us when the hunt was on. Fonso was out, we knew where, and Hubert was not with us, but we did not know where. We last saw him when the Burgundian Queen rode out in her black gown, with the black dwarf on a pony with her and Piet on foot leading a spare horse. It seemed to us that Rafe knew where Hubert was, but he could not say. Anyway, Roberto and I would play cards.

On the third hunt there was occasion for us to go. There was a bright cold day, and snow on the palace roof when we woke and drew back the old horse-skin. Our breath had hung solid on the roof of our place. Before the hunt was to leave a pavilion had to be set up five miles away. The pavilion was a golden tent as large as a banqueting hall, and it took all the menservants of the castle, and all the men from the village, to put it up, and it was taken in three carts at early dawn. We had heard it go before we woke. But by daylight we were to follow, because today was a court day, with dukes and counts coming to the King, and it was also the proper day for the King to welcome the Queen of Burgundy officially. He had been to her door and not been admitted, he had hunted with her, but she still was not welcomed as a queen.

In our cold, smelly kennel we put on thin fine clothes, and came out shivering into the sun. There was no thought that we should break our fast. We were to ride in a cart, or walk if that pleased us better, and help with the fitting out of the tent, and then wait the pleasure of whatever beast was hunted that day, and when it had agreed to die and the hunt was able to return, we were to be of the court.

Being of the court was our place and our duty, next in station below the Infanta, but not having any wisdom in state affairs. Rafe knew what was happening, and was made happy by it because he had new sorts of joke and mime ready for the King and the visiting Queen. We had seen him practising them (because he could not hear when we approached) and we knew they would be successful and that we should all be beaten for his cheek, after everyone, including the King, had laughed. We were not sure, this time, how much the Burgundian Queen would laugh; we were sure the dwarf woman Elise, and Bouk and Piet would not laugh at all.

Hubert was not pleased to go, but he had to. Strangely, he did not cheer himself up that day until he saw Bouk and Piet pass us by in the hunt, when it caught up with the cart. We did not know why he took pleasure in our natural enemies.

45

The hunt may last an hour, it may last a day. It depends on the foresters and it depends on what other matters the King has to deal with. So we were ready with the tent as soon as possible, even though the hunt could be heard only very far off and nothing had been scented and kept to pursue.

The tent was in the usual clearing in the forest, under a great grey cliff. Round it there were other tents and pavilions, and to the place came other noble huntsmen and their servants, some having arrived early or the day before, others coming late on the hunt day and setting out to follow if they could. We knew nearly all, because they came every year. This year some were French noblemen, no doubt coming because the Queen of part of their country was here and was a fearless huntswoman herself.

Then there came someone we dwarfs were pleased to see, and who could be our best help. Riding in among one of the best arrays of the day was a white-haired man with a little skull-cap of red cloth, and beside him were banners and guards, not hunting men, and with him there rode too a priest.

The priest was a chaplain, a servant to a greater man; the guards were defenders of the church; the banners were those of the country and of the Blessed Virgin, and the white-haired man was the Cardinal Archbishop, at whose feet all men fell on their knees until they were told to rise. We knelt as well as we could. You will understand that I have no knees in my legs and cannot kneel. But I have more sense in my head than the others. For a time, among all the kneeling servants and courtiers I was the tallest.

The Cardinal Archbishop was our friend, above all people. He had first noticed us when I could not kneel when he was a Bishop and a humble man. He had scolded me, but I showed him my legs, and he said it was God's will that at certain times I was not to be humble. Since then, now that he had found someone whom God had put above a Bishop's pride and office, he had become our friend. In the town he would come to our quarters, saying that he was humbled again by having to bend low, and talk to us, and stroke Fonso's head until he slept, and by

46

putting his hand on Rafe's throat would make him speak some few slow words (that Rafe would forget, since they were not Italian), and for the others of us, who are not afflicted greatly he would bring his love, and we would love him.

So we were pleased to see him at the pavilion, and hoped the hunt would find and find again and come late back so that we could speak with him. But that was not to be just then. The Cardinal Archbishop came near and spoke to us, asking after Fonso with a voice between a bell and the cry of a distant hound, and called each of us by name, and said we were his children, and that made Hubert sob and hold the Archbishop's hand.

"I shall be here more than a week," said the Archbishop. "I shall speak to the King, to the Burgundian Queen, to the sick people, and then to you." Hubert sniffed, smiled, wiped his eyes, and the Archbishop went on to his own pavilion.

There was no King to talk to until dusk. Then the great lamps were lighted within the golden pavilion, and the fires piled high and the meat set to roast. The King rode in smiling and weary. The Burgundian Queen followed in a little while, satisfied with her day too. As they came they both bowed to the pavilion of the Cardinal Archbishop. Then men washed and talked and servants carried water and basted the meat and the tables were set and there was coming and going. Fonso came back hand in hand with the Infanta, which offended the lady-in-waiting. Both children (because Fonso is a child) were trying to ride the dog, and shrieked and tumbled their way. The Infanta had come out in a coach, and this little distance had not made her ill. They had come upon Fonso in the middle of the track waiting with his dog for the hunt to return to the palace, which it had not done.

We thought that two more children had come in the next small party, but we had made half that mistake before. One child was not so, but was the Burgundian Queen's dwarf woman. The other was a boy of about twelve, walking with her, and overtopping her.

"He is the son of the Burgundian Queen," said Hubert.

"He is Charles, The Dolphin of Burgundy. We shall see him at supper in the gold pavilion. There is something afoot, Joachim; something we have not yet been told."

So there might be, I thought; but here today is high authority, the Cardinal Archbishop, and if there is a question that we dwarfs are to be sold out of the country (which was what I feared most of any change that could be made) then he will speak for us, and perhaps keep us himself.

Then we all went to supper, at the King's table, to which we belong. There were a King and Queen, and a Knave who was the Dolphin, who are high cards in our usual game, and the highest card, the Ace is God himself, and the next the ten, but above the King, was the Cardinal Archbishop, eating like a man and sounding like a bell; and below these great cards came those three favoured beings the Queen's dwarfs, completing the pack. The five of us King's dwarfs were the rejected cards of Brusquembille, the two, three, four, five, six; the Infanta, who is after all another Queen, makes a Bezique with the Dolphin, and that is our hand at the supper table.

6

If you put two dominoes end to end and then place one more between them to make a cross you will understand how the tables were set. The King was opposite the Queen on the short arms of the cross, and each of them sat alone at an end. The King had the Cardinal Archbishop along a side near him, and the Queen had her own court chaplain, who was nowhere near being even an ordinary bishop.

We dwarfs belong to the King's table, but we do not sit at it. We wait on the King, for whatever is needed. The Queen's dwarfs waited on her, the dwarf woman tending her napkin, holding it for her and having it always ready to be raised to the royal lips. Rafe saw this and made a long mimicking of it, and the little woman looked stonily at him. Roberto stayed by the King for some time, then wandered away and took himself outside in his red, thin, leather coat from Cordoba. I thought he might be thinking of a song and would do it better away from the crowd of royalty and nobility, perhaps by the cooking fires burning under the cliff outside. The cooking fires had been a marvel to watch, with their red light glowing out of the cliff, their smoke hanging higher up and shining red, the snow falling in front red and black and white, and the cooks like small black flames against the fire. In front of this spread of fire the golden pavilion was like something magical that floated in its own frail light.

Fonso, of course, was no great help at table. He went round the guests with the dog, begging for scraps, which were not for him but for the dog. Fonso would taste them, and if they were good the dog got them. If they were not to his liking he would eat them grudgingly, and if they were nothing he or the dog could eat he would gravely give the offering back.

I waited on the King with my own hands. Hubert was not at our side of the table at all, but over at the Queen's side. I supposed the King had sent him over so that each side had four dwarfs. Bouk and Piet were by the Queen, doing very little but drink and now and then lounge up to the Queen's chaplain and speak some words to him in a superior way, as if they were more important than he was. They probably were, because the Burgundian court was a small one, and the dwarfs seemed too proud of themselves. We, of course, were proud of our court first, and of ourselves last. But at the same time we had to look out for ourselves, as you will know, because people like Don Emilio thought we were of no account at all, neither feeding us nor telling us of what was going on.

Roberto had not been told what was going on, he tells me. He had simply guessed. I had not thought of it in the slightest, and Hubert had other things on his mind. But the hunt supper, when it was almost over, began to feel different from other hunt suppers. It was not the first time we had had another reigning monarch present, either on a friendly visit or because he had been captured in some war. We had no greater number of noblemen present than usual, and no greater number of ladies, since there was usually our own Queen, now dead, and some countesses who came, and sometimes another foreign Queen with her husband. This was the first time we had had the Cardinal Archbishop here, though. He was enjoying it, with a big basket of fire at his back to warm him, and his own chaplain to bring him to eat and drink and his red skull cap to keep his head warm.

But there was something different. At one point in the

meal the doors opened and there came in four armed knights who were not true knights. We knew them as winter palace guards, and they were acting foolishly in their armour and helmets, giving each other salutes that meant nothing, like men playing at being officers and knowing nothing about it, like little girls playing at being queens and giving haughty orders and knowing nothing about it. These men stood about in the pavilion, a little nervous, not going too near a brazier.

Our little girl, the Infanta, was not being haughty or pretending to be a queen. She had eaten her supper, a boiled egg, followed by a lot of bread and gravy, and was yawning on her tall chair and tending to put her feet on the table when the lady-in-waiting was not looking. She was also sucking her thumb and picking her nose.

The other child, Charles, the Dolphin of Burgundy, sat opposite the Infanta, next to the Queen's chaplain. These two children looked at each other very often, because they were two of a kind, but they were both bored with the long supper. Though I am proud of my court, I will say that the Dolphin behaved better than the Infanta, yet she is only six years old.

Then the whole table went silent, at no signal I could see. There was some rattling of knives and glasses for a moment, and the four soldiers dressed as knights stood still and stopped clattering their side arms and vizors and stood up like men.

The King stood up. Everybody else stood up hastily, and then sat down again when the King told them to. The Infanta, during the confusion of moving benches, threw bread at the Dolphin, and when she was scolded by the lady-in-waiting she slid away under the table and went round plaguing peoples' feet, particularly the King's.

I thought the King was only to say how well the hunt had done and what it was to do the next day. But it was not that at all. He said that all the people there knew already — all but the men of his own table, was the truth — what he was to say, and that he now had to say it with his own mouth and hear any objections, and that he was prepared for them. At this the four soldiers shuffled and rattled.

I began to remember hearing something like this ten or twelve years before, because I have been at the court for many years. But the King said it again before I could recall it.

"I declare," he said, "in the face of all men present, and before almighty God" (bowing to the Cardinal Archbishop, the ten of the suit though not the Ace) "that I intend to take to wife in all honour and as Queen of my country, Mathilde, now Queen of Burgundy." And at this all the faces that had been watching him swung together and looked at the Queen. And as well, just in that moment, the Dolphin, probably invited by the Infanta, slid under the table with her.

The Cardinal Archbishop stood up then, and spoke. I heard him, but did not watch him. I was watching Rafe and the King. Rafe had seen the faces move from King to Queen, and seen the silence continue, and wanted to be told what it meant.

"Ye have heard," said the Archbishop, ducking his head at each word as if he had to swing the tongue of a little bell in his throat for each separate word, "our sovereign Lord the King make declaration of his intent to take to wife the honourable majesty of the Queen of Burgundy. I call upon all men to declare now, in their turn, whether there be any reason known to them against the proposed matrimony, before God, or against the State, or by any reason of Honour. If any man has cause against the King in this matter he must stand forth now and settle."

One of the soldiers in knight's uniform stood out then, not quite standing forward but being abandoned by the others. "I declare," he said, in a thick Barcelona accent, "against the King." Then one of the others kicked him for forgetting his line. "In honour," he added, and pulled out his sword.

"I offer my champion to defend my honour," said the King, sitting down now. He was after all in the middle of telling Rafe what he and the Queen were intending to do.

The King's champion was one of the other soldiers, and he came forward and began to fight very woodenly, like the badly arranged combats in the street plays in the town at Epiphany, banging their wooden swords against each other.

At length, in this fight, the soldier who had declared against the King held up his arm carefully, and the champion, with as much care, pushed the point of his sword into it, lifting up his visor so that he could do it thoroughly and see the blood. That meant the challenger was defeated, and it was true that at the sudden spurt he lifted his own visor, turned the colour of grease, and dropped down in a faint. His opponent carried him out, laughing, and saying "Poor old 'Mberto, hold on lad, it's only a drop, no need to turn it up like that."

Meanwhile the Queen's priest, the simple chaplain, was getting up and making the speech the Archbishop had made, but making it for the Queen. The Queen was saying nothing at this time but listening to a long and angry argument full of much hand-waving from Elise, the dwarf woman, who was exceedingly cross, and who ended the speech by sulkily turning her back on the majesty of Burgundy and muttering privately to Hubert, who was still over at that side.

The clownish soldiers were pushing each other forward and making their clumsy and ill-remembered speeches. But, pushing through them, there came another indignant dwarf, who was Roberto, and he was to be against the Queen's honour, and challenged her for a champion.

Bouk and Piet, at the Queen's side, were coming forward to be her champions, but Hubert (who was the King's dwarf, after all) was there first, and stepping up on to the table over the Dolphin's chair, and putting his feet among the dishes. He had to be on the table to find his weapons. Roberto was armed with a sharp wooden skewer from the cooking fires, and the iron lid of some stew-pot for a shield. Hubert picked up the pot lid of a spice jar and the shank bone from a sheep, picked bare on a dish. He did not forget his duty of humour, and before the fighting began, as Roberto was helped on to the table by two barons, he dipped the shank end in mustard.

All the watching company, except the King, thought this was a mere entertainment, but I, knowing my two companions, knew that each of them meant the fight to be serious, but I did not know why.

53

The clumsy soldiers were distracted from their mock battle, over behind the Queen's chair. They gaped at the two on the table, and did not look at what they were doing, so that in their case the challenger won by thrusting his sword in the other's leg, who swore and was helped out into the cold and snow, and no more was known about them.

The two fighting dwarfs came to the middle of the table and faced one another across a dish of custard. The company round the table had eaten enough, and ignored the food on the board, but their glasses and their carafes of wine were brought to the edge of the table, into safety.

The fight began. It was serious indeed, and each of them was trying to hurt the other first. To hurt first they had to hit first, because the first blood drawn settled the matter. Often, however, a fight went on longer than it need, because both sides were warmed up to the affair. This fight was one that could go on *à outrance*, to the natural end with one dead.

It was club and pot against skewer and lid, and to those who did not know it was a well-timed piece of entertainment. But I knew it was not that, and I did not know what it was.

I came to the King, after a little time, since he was doing nothing, and Rafe was watching the table top with a long face, not finding, like me, anything agreeable in what he saw.

"Sire," I said, "what is this fight?"

"Joachim, my friend," said the King, "you have much sense when you know what is going on, but sometimes to bring you to understand what you can plainly see is beyond any of us."

"I am only a misshapen dwarf," I said, because that is true. "And I only wish to understand."

"It is this," said the King. "Roberto understands that when the Queen and I are married then there will be eight dwarfs, and perhaps that is too many, and the Queen and I will not keep them all."

"I understand, Sire," I said, because now Roberto's part was clear.

"It is a great household," said the King. "Do you not think?" I nodded, as much as I am able. "Perhaps", said the King, "there should not be so many dwarfs; perhaps Roberto should be made Chancellor, and you, Joachim, the Chamberlain or even an Archbishop." But at this I knew the King was joking, though what he said about Roberto was true. And I still did not know about Hubert and why he should take the Queen's part.

The fight had gone up and down the table now. Roberto had stepped in the custard, and Hubert had trampled a snowdrift of rice, but so far the only blood spilt was gravy. The two royal children had heard the pounding on the boards over their heads and had stopped plaguing feet, probably after getting a kick or two from people who assumed they were dogs. They now came up in each others' places, the Dolphin next to the lady-in-waiting, and the Infanta next to the Queen's chaplain. The chaplain talked to her, and she threw nuts at him, and went under the table again. She came out in her own place and the Dolphin came out in his, and they threw nuts at each other.

The lady-in-waiting took the Infanta's hand and began to talk to her. I was just behind, and I heard her saying first that one should behave in front of one's court, and the Infanta would not admit it. Then the lady-in-waiting started talking in sentimental and excited tones about the Infanta's new Mama, the Burgundian Queen, and the Infanta, after looking at the Queen and then at her father, and understanding that something in her life had changed, very likely for the worse, became angry and started to scratch the lady-in-waiting. The lady-in-waiting was used to that, and always kept the Infanta's nails very short. The Infanta spat at her, then at the Queen, and threw the last walnut at her, but of course it went astray. The Infanta was plainly upset, but I could not tell why, just as I could not tell why Hubert was fighting Roberto.

The fight came along the table now. The Infanta acted without cunning, just out of mischief of one sort or another, when she grabbed Hubert the Queen's champion from behind, getting him behind the knees with both

55

hands and pulling him back. She is bigger than Hubert. He staggered, dropped his pot shield and his bone, and grabbed at the nearest thing, which was Roberto's skewer. I acted quickly then, because I could see the end of the fight if I did. I pulled the back of the Infanta's chair, and tipped it over on to the ground. She came with it, and Hubert on top of her, and on top of him Roberto, and the lady-in-waiting. Underneath them all was Joachim, me, with my stiff legs unable to move away from my own trick. And the fight ended with no blood spilt, only a great deal of salad oil and fruit and cheese and butter and some heavy Portuguese wine the colour and price of blood.

7

The Cardinal Archbishop came striding up beside our cart
in the snow. We were all five in it most of the time. Now
and then Fonso would leap out into a soft-looking heap of
snow and wrestle with the dog, and I would have to stop
the cart and have him dragged in. I have to be in the cart
because I cannot walk five miles in the day. Roberto was
nursing a lamed ankle from yesterday's fighting among
the puddings; Hubert was bruised only, and that mostly
from landing underneath the lady-in-waiting when I had
tipped up the chair. Rafe rode along with me. All of us
were quiet but Fonso. It was strange that he and Hubert
should seem happy, and the others of us had nothing but
bad to expect of the future.

I stopped the cart for the Archbishop. He is another
simple person like Fonso, but differently simple, and only
for truly simple people do I stop the cart. The Archbishop
would not come up on board, though there was room
against the folds of the pavilion, gold cold and wet at our
backs.

We welcomed his Grace as well as we could. We are not
simple (except Fonso) but neither are we gracious; we are
God's plain creatures. His Grace walked alongside us and
we leaned on the side of the cart and told him many
things; how we had come out here before the court as if we

were banished, how Don Emilio had treated us with no respect, and at this the Archbishop made no comment but waited in silence until we told him how we treated Don Emilio with no respect too, and had stolen from him.

"But you are sorry now," said His Grace. "You are repentant and you will no longer steal," and we said that it might be so, and the Archbishop said he would bless us but could not grant forgiveness for a continuing sin until we were repentant. So he stayed with us an hour, and before he went he left us his great cloak to cover ourselves, saying he had another like it among his vestments. However, before he went we had told him all our sorrows past, of evil lodgings and unkindly deeds, and our sorrows for the future, of how we might be put out into the world alone, or sold to other uncaring Kings, even perhaps to Africa. The Archbishop said that he would speak to the King about all these matters, as soon as the wedding was done the next day.

During the day the courtyard of the palace filled up with carts and coaches and wagons and rows of horses, until at the last there was no way of walking through, so great was the tangle. Don Emilio at last insisted on a path from the gateway to the door of the state apartments, where the wedding was to be, but that was too late for the safety of some carriage shafts, and there was broken wood and fierce anger before the day was done.

The snow had fallen since morning. From each chimney of the castle, all day long, there rose smoke, like a town. All day long, sifting down in the snow, there came grey ash, black charcoal and sometimes fire turning to steam. By nightfall the grey snow lying smoothed on the stilled traffic in the yard had turned white under lantern-light and all was like a box of shrivelled fruits and dry leaves bleached white and inhabited by glow-worms.

The Infanta had come out during the day with her lady-in-waiting, wrapped into a roundness that could hardly walk. To get at the snow, which she wanted to throw at people, she had to lie down, and of course that was wrong, and she screamed all the way back to the castle, taking snow from carriage wheels and throwing it in the lady-in-waiting's face, who said that one should not behave like that, should one. Roberto got in one good shot at Don Emilio who was passing through the yard then, and who thought it must be the Infanta's snowball, and smiled forgivingly at her.

"Another time there will be a stone in it," said Roberto. He and I were alone. Our friends the King's servants had put us out of the State Apartments, where they were making ready for the wedding. Rafe had managed to stay quietly there, watching. Fonso was engaged in a long game with the dog, which really wanted to be in the kitchen asleep. Hubert was nowhere to be found, again.

There were good pickings that night from the kitchen. We were able to waylay the dishes as they came back cold from the tables in the various parts of the palace, and take a share to our part of it, the hole in the wall next to the dogs. We ate without Hubert, who only came to us at a very late hour and would not say where he had been, but seemed happy to have been there. Roberto studied him by the light of our stolen candles, and said nothing, but he had some thought in his mind and would not share it.

Afterwards, on account of what Hubert had heard on some occasion he would not tell us of, we went to the State Apartments and watched from a stairway how the King and Queen and their attendants and the Archbishop with his, went through the form of the wedding service; seeing how one person should now stand, and how another should walk here or there; and how the King should take the Queen's hand. Among the attendants were the Infanta and the Dolphin, following the bride. But the Infanta would not play this game for the new Queen. She would be part of some other work, and go in a procession, but she would do nothing for this bride. For some few steps she would walk beside the Dolphin, and then she would take herself away in a quiet sulk, and if possible would take the Dolphin too. When the Queen spoke to her she turned her back and screamed, and at last she was sent to bed.

The wedding took place in the middle of the next day. Of the guests, those that had to come very far were already here. Those that came from nearer at hand were able to arrive for the middle of the day and leave with daylight for travelling. The new arrivals came walking in all morning, their diligences left far outside the palace. They came dressed in cloak and snow, and suddenly were brightly clothes below. We five were all at the State Apartment doors in a vile draught taking wet cloaks and heaping them in an anteroom. Then there were four of us, because Fonso went to sleep under the cloaks, and we left him there in case he forgot himself in some way during the wedding. Then there were three, because Hubert had gone again, and said nothing. But by then the visitors were here and were in the Apartments ready to witness. We three went up a cold spiral stair and out into a small gallery and looked down on the assembly.

The room was lit by candles, and the windows were gloomy. The King waited by a pillar, every now and then glancing back to a doorway. Then the Archbishop, who was by the altar put here for that day alone to make the room into a holy church, turned to look to that door himself, and walked towards it. It opened, and as it did so a sign came from God in a lightening of the windows by a shaft of sunshine, so that the windows were for a time the equal of the candles. The Queen came out, and she was dazzling with her red and gold hair and the sun, even under her veil, and the firm majesty of her bearing. After her came her son, the Dolphin, bearing a train. With him for a moment came the Infanta, being pushed by the lady-in-waiting, the woman dwarf, and, of all people, Hubert, who was once more in the Queen's household.

The Infanta would not come. It was to do with the Queen, who took no notice; it was nothing to do with the crowd of people, because the Infanta loves a crowd and is not shy. The door closed on her scream, and the Queen walked down the room attended by one boy, who was perhaps not used to so many people, and who looked behind him more than once in the hope that the Infanta would come. She did not. She stayed behind the closed door and could be heard shouting and storming.

The wedding was plain enough. For the first time we

heard the Queen speak in a firm voice, and the familiar voice of the King, saying what I had once before heard him say, and the voice of our own Archbishop and friend, ringing out unsteadily but finishing each phrase fully.

Then that was all over, and the altar candles were put out, and that altar could not be used again after that day, and the room would no longer be a royal chapel but one where anything might happen. The King and his Queen went to the Throne Room and the visitors went past that way to greet them. The King was on his own throne, but the Burgundian Queen was not yet Queen in this country, and could not sit on the Queen's throne. Instead she sat neatly on a stool beside the King, and we all went by and kissed his hand and hers and the great red ring of the Cardinal Archbishop, and went on to the wedding breakfast.

At this meal the King and Queen sat together, and that brought all of us (including Fonso, when Roberto had woken him and brought him) together again. But Hubert clearly stayed with the Queen's side of the household, which puzzled me, and made Piet and Bouk angry. But Hubert did not care to notice them.

The Infanta did not come to her place, beside the Dolphin. But he missed her, and went at last to fetch her, and got her nearly to the place made for her and then she saw it was near the Queen and would come no further. But the Dolphin was a boy twice her age and much bigger, and he picked her up all at once, whether she liked it or not, and put her in her chair and gave her a punishing thump as he did. At that she cried, turned her back on the Queen, pulled the Dolphin's hair, drank some milk put ready for her, and leaned on her new friend.

But she would not speak to the King, her father, or the Queen, and pouted at them both and cried, and had to be coaxed to eat by the Dolphin. When it was time for her to be taken away during the afternoon she was not pleased again, being only a little girl of six and not liking change. She did not appeal to the King or the Queen, of course, or to any of us dwarfs, which is what she might easily have done. She asked the Dolphin to speak for her, and held his

61

hand. The Dolphin was not sure he wanted her still beside him because he was now speaking to the Duke of Endyre's son, who was as much older than him as he was older than the Infanta. He solved it in a gentlemanly way, making an excuse to the Duke's son, a bow to the King and another to the Queen, and he escorted the Infanta to the door, and by the time she had got there the lady-in-waiting had begun on some story that satisfied her and she went through listening to her.

The King and Queen rose, and stood. That was a sign for the guests to be going if they wished. We went to the door and gave back the cloaks and coats. Piet and Bouk came to help with this work, and so did Hubert for a time. When all had gone who were going, we went back to the table and found the King and Queen and a company of friends, and for ourselves plenty of good eating again; it was like the old days of plenty at the town palace the years before when King and Queen were always entertaining. Perhaps those days had come again.

The Archbishop left his place and came down to us, all five. "If you think it wise, my friends, I shall now speak with the King about all your problems," he said. "But first, show me where you are now lodged."

We took him out among the carriages of the yard, no longer silent and still, but shifting and noisy with the voices of drivers, and showed him our cave in the wall. When he came back with us he stood before the King and interceded for us. He said he knew the King would not want us to be in discomfort or to come to harm, and he recounted all that we had told him of Don Emilio's doings, and at that very time Don Emilio was there, drinking with the King, but gradually drinking less, because all that we had told the Archbishop in truth was being told by him to the King.

At the end the King was silent. Indeed, I believe his wits were scattered for the time being with wine. But he spoke at last, and told Don Emilio to stand and listen, because he was one servant among many and had not to put himself before others, or lower other servants or members of the King's household. Then Don Emilio told the King what

62

the Archbishop had not said, how we had stolen and not been perfect fellow-servants.

The King laughed at that and spread out his hands. "In one hand I find unkindness," he said, "and in the other I find a little poaching, a little thieving, a little malice. I do not know which hand is the heavier, I do not know which hand is the lighter. I say you have all spoken out now, and the matter is even between you."

"But my friends have evil lodgings," said the Archbishop. "If your Majesty will not find them better then I shall sleep there myself, and let my friends take my bed – it will fit them." He looked round at us then and measured us with his eye, and would have been wrong because only four of us stood there: Hubert had gone again.

"I will see these lodgings, Lord Bishop," said the King. "No matter is too great or too small for me on my wedding day. Come, Joachim, lead the way; come, Don Emilio; come, Fonso," and the dog came and licked his hand.

The Queen waited, looking round for her dwarf woman Elise, but she had gone away from the room and the Queen had to do without. Piet and Bouk served her instead.

I led the way to the door, and to the yard. "It is of no account, Sire," I said to the King. "It is neither large nor small; it is nothing."

"Do not impede justice," said the King, and we went on. "First, however, we shall see how Don Emilio lodges himself. Don Emilio, you shall now lead the way."

So the King went into Don Emilio's house at the back of the barbican and Donna Emilio was heard to shriek with surprise, and we saw her talking with the King wearing one shoe and not the other and wearing an old torn shawl and with her hair knotted with string to curl it. She had thought she was safe from interruption with Don Emilio at the King's table.

The King came out of the lodgings and came down along the wall to where we had been put. Before he got there he asked to see where we had been before, and we turned about and went down to our old place in the colonnade under the terrace. Here stood all the furnishings of Bouk and Piet, and there burnt the fire, and all was set out very well. So we knew that, by accident, the King would think we had done very badly to be put in a hole in the wall.

There was a candle burning inside, behind the horse-skin, as we came there through the snow. Roberto climbed the wall the little way necessary to come at the opening, and pulled back the curtain.

In the little room sat the missing Hubert, and upon his knee was the dwarf woman, who had been missing too. She was holding his head and kissing him, and he was kissing her and clasping her tight round the waist.

"Evening one and all," said Hubert, letting her go. She leapt up and looked angry. "Thought I'd be found out sooner or later." Then he saw it was the King looking in. "Oh Crikey," he said. Then the Archbishop came closer. "Oh Lumme," said Hubert.

"My Lord Bishop," says the King, "do dwarfs then love?"

"Sire," says the Archbishop, "do Kings?"

"It is not unknown," says the King. "Good master priest, they shall be kings and queens too, in their day. But first I shall do what I came out to do."

He had come to look at our little room in the wall, and that was what he did. Hubert picked up the candle and stood with it. The dwarf woman stood beside him, and then was overcome by being discovered at all and overwhelmed by the King and the Cardinal Archbishop. She ran forward and would have jumped down the wall and out under their feet, like a cornered cat wanting to be in her room. But the King caught her with one hand and she stood still, stiffened like iron and ready to run.

"Not so quickly away, lady," said the King.

"Stay here, daughter," said the Archbishop. "The King has not come seeking you."

"I had thought," said the King, letting go the horse skin at the door of our lodging, "I had thought to send Don Emilio here for the night, for what he thinks good enough for my household is surely good enough for him. But this place is too mean, and even a King must have mercy. I shall blame him greatly, and he shall give up his own bed and his own rooms, and sleep where he likes. But he will see that even I will not send men to sleep in a hole in a wall. Lord Bishop, speak with these two, and when you have spoken and done what you think right we shall be pleased to hear of it."

And the King walked off alone, leaving us with the Archbishop in the snow. Elise began to sob into her sleeve. Hubert came to the edge of the hole and sat there, and a snowflake fell spluttering into the candle. "Now love," he said, reaching down a hand to Elise and patting her shoulder. "Nothing will happen to you."

"I will speak to these two," said the Archbishop. "Joachim, my friend, take the others back to the State Apartment and wait for us."

We left them, and the Archbishop was saying as we went that he could not haul his old bones up into the wall, and that Hubert and Elise should come under his cloak, and Hubert was saying, "Cut it out, girl," to the still-sobbing Elise.

We waited in the cold empty room for some time, not knowing what to do. We had a candle, and we had our pack of cards, but this room was now no playroom but a chapel with a holy altar, a church. So we sat on the carpet and wondered what could happen to Hubert and Elise, because surely they would both be sent away in disgrace, because in spite of the King's question and the Cardinal's answer it was not known that a dwarf should love; all that is wanted from him is loyalty and service and what his wits will provide.

"There is a song in this," said Roberto, and began to pluck it out on the guitar, that hearts were warm in snow, but snow melts and the heart freezes, and it is all hopeless.

There was one candle. There were more on the altar, but we could not light their gospel or epistle. That would have been wrong. But before long the door of the room opened and the Archbishop came in. We thought he was alone, but when he had taken our single candle and lit the two on the altar we saw Hubert step out from under the snowy cloak.

"Roberto," said the Archbishop, "stay with Hubert. He has need of a man with him now."

66

"For reasons of Church, State, and Honour," said Hubert. "Tell me a simple prayer, Roberto, and kneel by me. The Cardinal Archbishop would have me too freshly clean for what is to come, but you will give me a dwarf's benediction."

"Joachim," said the Archbishop, "my chaplain is talking to the Infanta's lady-in-waiting. Will you ask him to come to me here, and will you ask her royal highness to send the little ring that is on the second finger of her right hand that was given to her when she visited the shrine of Saint James at Easter."

I took this errand to the Infanta's rooms, and found the chaplain there, and gave my message. But the lady-in-waiting, who does not often notice me, told me to stay and tell her why I was troubled. I was not troubled, I said, but she showed me that tears ran down my face, and I had not seen them.

"The Archbishop sends for a ring from the Infanta," I said, and the Infanta put out her hand proudly to show the rings. "It is this," I said, pointing it out. The Infanta did not want to give it up, but the Archbishop was someone she had to obey. While she pulled it off her finger, where it was well on, the lady-in-waiting made me drink wine and tell her my trouble. At last I did tell her the thing I hardly dare think, that I thought Hubert was to be executed, and that the Archbishop was now getting him ready in his mind for losing his head.

"But has the Archbishop sent for one's rope or one's axe?" said the lady-in-waiting. "No, he has sent for one's ring. Perhaps Hubert is to be," and here she pealed with laughter because the thought was very ridiculous to her, "perhaps Hubert is to be married."

Of course, then I knew it was so, that Hubert was to be married, and in the State Apartment and by the Archbishop, just as the King and the new Queen had been, and I told the lady-in-waiting so.

"No," she said, covering her face, "one has not laughed. One sees that Hubert is more a man than the King is, because there are few kings but many dwarfs. So one has been foolish to laugh, you hear, your highness."

"I will come too," said the Infanta. "Are we all to be King and Queen tonight?"

We came down, out of the warm nursery rooms to the cold high hall, me, the chaplain, the lady-in-waiting, the Infanta, and two dolls that were in favour.

Hubert and Roberto had said their prayer and stood down in the darkness. The Archbishop had taken off his cloak and once more was in his wedding vestments, with the candles gleaming golden on the embroidery. Roberto was dusting straw from Hubert and telling him not to shake and scolding him for spoiling a new song. The Infanta went to the Archbishop and gave him her hand for him to take the ring, but he sent her to Roberto with it. Fonso and the dog went to lie on the cushions at the altar rail, one either side of the gate. The chaplain went to put on his plain church clothes and bring the bishop's staff to the Cardinal Archbishop, and to stand beside him with the cross. And we waited for the bride.

"I would have music here," said Roberto. "I would say how the snow falls miserably on the hills and it is winter, and then it melts and there is spring all at once over the whole country, on King and man and dwarf."

"Sing it then," said the Archbishop. "But ascribe it to God. But not now," because the door had opened again and Elise had come in, "sing it later." The Archbishop and his chaplain went down the aisle to meet the bride.

She was unattended and very small, and walked through darkness until the lady-in-waiting took a candle and went to her, and would have attended her. But the Infanta ran ahead of her, brushing past the Archbishop, and pushed her aside, and did what she should have done that afternoon, taking up the trailing end of a wedding robe and carrying it, being the bridesmaid.

Then the door thudded softly once more, and more people were in the dark end of the room, and suddenly Elise had another attendant. The Queen's son, the Dolphin of Burgundy, had come to attend her too, as a page. Elise turned and clasped him for a moment, and it was plain that a dwarf can love. To the Infanta she curtsied, and the Infanta curtsied back in her childish way and

68

tumbled over. But she picked herself up and went on.

Someone came and stood behind us – behind me and Rafe. I heard Rafe sniff and smell them. Bouk and Piet were there, and behind them two other presences in the darkness.

The bride and her attendants came to the head of the aisle. Here Hubert and Roberto joined them, and once more that day the wedding service began, and the same man that married King to Queen married dwarf to dwarf.

Beside me the lady-in-waiting sobbed and said that one found it so beautiful. Further back, where I could not see, another woman wept in the same way, as if she were the bride's mother, for that is what they do.

Then it was over, and there was the book to sign, where before only Kings and Queens had been registered. The chaplain wrote out the page with his own hand, and witnessed Hubert's mark, because no one had taught Hubert to write. The new wife wrote her own name with her own hand. "I will teach you," she said, and kissed Hubert, unashamed now before us at the altar rail. Then Fonso must needs sign the book with his own hand, a graceful cross, and the Infanta'less gracefully all across the page, and the Cardinal Archbishop last. The book was laid open to let the ink dry, and we came from the altar, bringing its candles with us, candles that had been at two weddings.

By their light we now saw that the King and the Queen had been there too, and it was the Queen who had wept as if Elise were her own child. As we went out towards them Bouk and Piet came out from their places and solemnly put up their swords into an arch and let the bride and groom go under, and their attendants, and the Archbishop waited and held the candle for them.

Then the King himself led them to the Throne room and set them on two footstools and with his own hand he made the fire greater and brought cake and wine for everyone, and he and the Queen sat as they had in the afternoon and called for a toast to married lives and happiness to himself and his Queen and to Hubert and his wife. We drank the toast.

And there we were, the Ace of the pack, that is God, guiding us all to this happy end; the next card the Cardinal Archbishop, the ten, coming above the King and his Queen the Royal Marriage, and after the Royal Marriage the Ordinary Marriage (and consider that an Ordinary Marriage is twenty points scored, and a Royal Marriage no more than twice that, forty, so there is no great difference). The King kissed the Queen, and there they were happy; Hubert kissed Elise, and there they were happy too, and we of the rest of the pack were happy with them, and the Dolphin came to kiss his mother for her pleasure, and after him came the Infanta, no longer angry with pride. Then the Infanta went shyly off beyond the fireplace with the Dolphin, who did not know what was to come to him.

"I love him best of all," said the Infanta, clutching her two dolls and the Dolphin equally, but she kissed the Dolphin, not the dolls, and he gravely returned the kiss. They were the Bezique to our game, or, in our language here, the *besico*, or little kiss.

BOY TO ISLAND

1

At the new moon of September the boats cross the sea to the island, Faransay, and bring in the lambs for the Strath market.

The men were down on the strand when Colin Henderson went up the hillside with the cows. His dog Cathal ran about. The cows knew how to follow the path without his help.

"You will wish you were going, Colin," said Anabel Tivert, when the cows she was driving had stood, looked at Colin's cows and ambled across to join them, snorting at Cathal on the way.

"Why shall I wish?" said Colin. He was looking down the hill, past the little round-backed houses, through their smoke, and over the beach to the boats. There was a new wild track over the pebbles and the sand, where five men, one of them his father, had brought down from a building four turbulent and fierce tups, or rams, to go to Faransay for the winter. The tups were tied in pairs by their horns, and each had a back leg hobbled to a foreleg. They could not go far wrong, but they would not go at all right. Now they were at the boats, being lifted in and tied down, so they would not kick, or stand to put hoof or horn through the leather bottom. Beyond the boats was the sea, and beyond that the island of Faransay, like a lamp in the mists, light and shadow.

Colin thought of the smell of the tallow fat on the boatskin, and of the staring square eyes of the rams. He thought of being close to the boats, of being in them.

"You will not be of an age to go yet," said Anabel.

"You are younger, and a girl," said Colin. "You will not go either."

"I shall go," said Anabel. "I am to give the Gift. I have been told today."

The Gift was the present for the people of the island, who were not talked about openly for fear of ill-luck.

"I am glad for you," said Colin, but he felt jealous and unhappy not to go himself, and he did not like Anabel at any time, though she often came and stood near him. "Take the cows up the hill. I am going to the boats. Cathal, come away."

He went down to his own house. "Well, mother," he said, "am I not to go sheep-herding?"

His mother knitted out her row that was not long, and looked across her stitches, that they were right. She rocked the cradle where the baby Donal lay.

"You will do better here at home," she said, "to mind the fireside and the cows. Next year the new moon comes again, and the market days. This year the boats are full. Your father and your uncle take the work."

"How long before I am a man?" said Colin. "Is it always bairns' work I am to do?"

"Nine years are not many," said his mother. "A man will bear what comes and not complain."

Colin said no more. The wind, or a bitter smoke from the fire, walked across his eye and made it smart as if a tear would fall. But he knew it would not, and could not.

"Alasdair sent a message," said his mother, at the end of another row. "You must be with him this morning to learn something, but he did not say what. It must be soon, because he goes to the island."

"It is making a reed for the bagpipe," said Colin. "I have had sticks drying by the fireside."

His mother missed a stitch or two in her row. "I had forgotten that," she said.

"They are to be dry," said Colin. He went down on his knees by the fire. The lengths of elderwood he had laid by the hearth-stone were not there. They had been taken for firewood and burnt.

"He will be vexed," said Colin. "Indeed he will. He will box my ears and see bad things for us all."

"Some time in the dark I laid that wood on," said his mother. "It was elderwood. I have laid misfortune on us, so what shall we do for the best?"

By now they were both thinking the same thought. Above the place of the fire in the wall, and over the door of the house, hung boughs of elder, to stop troubles and ills crossing the threshold and living indoors. Over the fireplace the sticks were dry.

"I will draw one out," said his mother. "And no one in the world, mortal or not, shall ever know, and no harm will come from it."

She drew one out, stripped the withered leaves from it, and gave it to Colin. She went back to her row of stitches, and rocked the baby with her foot.

Colin went to Alasdair's house. The old man was inside, and the fire in his tobacco pipe seemed larger than the one in his hearth.

"Is that kindling or reed furniture?" he said.

"It is dry stuff for a reed," said Colin.

"We will be in the house," said Alasdair. He had white hair, and his moustache flowed across his beard. "I am lame today. I have been a man too long, and old age is hardest to bear. Ah yes, that is a straight stick, and a dry one. First we shall cut a length," and he laid his knife across the stick between the places where the leaves hang. "Now, your knife to cut the other. Yes, that is it."

When the stick was cut, three inches long, the mealy pith from the middle had to be taken away with a splinter drawn from the remainder of the elderwood. When it was hollow Alasdair blew out the dust.

"The reed is to be cut," he said. "I will show you what like." He opened a box. It was full of little sticks. He took one up, and put it in his mouth, breathed through it, and it spoke, like the call of some bird. He did not put the reed to

73

his lips and blow, but had it inside his mouth. Colin took it and blew it the same way. It touched the back of his throat and made his stomach heave.

"It is not for the mouth," said Alasdair. "It is for a mouthpiece, and a quiet practice chanter with a single reed, that can be borne in the house. Now, Colin, look at the reed, and see how the cut is made, how the tongue is formed. And now you have seen, you must cut for yourself."

The cut on the first reed was poor, worse than Alasdair expected. He gave Colin a buffet with his fist, and Colin gathered his wits. He had been listening out towards the boats, instead of minding the knife. So the second time he made a better cut. Alasdair handed him wax and told him to stop up one end of the reed, then try it in his mouth.

That one would not speak, but the third one did. Alasdair put it in a flute-like chanter, with the mouthpiece over it, and sounded notes. "Well enough," he said. "Fetch me wood, boy, I cannot walk up the hill today."

"How shall you be on the island?" said Colin.

"I shall not go," said Alasdair. "I have been sixty and more times, and I lost my girl there that I was to marry, for she never came back, and now I am too old."

"I shall go instead," said Colin. "Even if Anabel will sit against me. But it is not likely."

"It is likely," said Alasdair. "I had word with your father. Well, if you are taking your little sticks with you, remember and do not play the pipes there, or you will be disturbing the inhabitants. Listen instead, and perhaps you will hear the four airts of a tune, which you must have, for every piper has to make his own tunes, or what has he given to the music?"

74

2

Colin's father was down by the boat still. He had been in the water, and his red trews were darkened with it above the knee. Colin's uncle, Duncan, was with him, waiting to be told what to do. Duncan could not hear or speak in this world, but there were sounds in his head and he would make them with his mouth. Sometimes the sounds were like a drum and people said he could hear fighting. Now he was watching Colin's father.

Colin ran to the boat, and waited until his father turned to see him. "Alasdair is lame, and I am to go in his place," Colin said. "Is that so, father?"

His father waited a little before answering, "We shall go nowhere until the water has lifted the boat from the shore." Then he spoke to Duncan: "Water must come under the boat." He lifted his hands to show what he meant.

Duncan agreed, cradling the boat of one hand in the sea of the other.

"And the weather?" said Colin's father. Duncan knew the weather. He looked near and far, up and down, felt the wind, sniffed, touched the sand, dipped a hand in the water, watched the birds in higher air, and then gave his signs to say that there would be a slight breeze the day with showers, a dry night, with mist in the morning, frost on the hills, and a new moon.

"But," said Colin, "am I to come?"

"You will bring the old plaid and a shepherd wallet," said his father. "Now Duncan," he went on, leaving the matter, "we need cheese, and oatmeal, and the fastenings for the lambs ..." There was no more now to be said to Colin.

But Colin had heard enough. His heart grew up in him like the bag of a set of pipes, and he could feel that a tune of delight was ready to whistle from his throat; his fingers longed to play, his legs to dance.

But a man, he thought, does not say it now. Perhaps later he will make a song about it, if any place gives him a tune. But for now he will remember it, and in front of the rest of the world lay it aside.

So when he came into the house again he said only, "I shall be needing the old plaid, mother, and a shepherd wallet."

"And a wool hat and a knit waistcoat," said his mother. "Is Duncan by the boat?" Duncan was her brother.

"He is telling the weather," said Colin.

"You will take his plaid and wallet too," said his mother. "Be outside first and bring me a week's turf for the fire. You are dandling there up and down like a spider. You can fill all your bed-stead with turf, and if it is still here when you come back you must take it out again."

Later on the two boats were floating. The sea had lifted under them. Until then no one had been let into them, because of their light, stretched construction. Now, men and women were wading back and forth, putting in the goods that would be needed on Faransay.

Mrs MacDonald came down to the shore from her house with the slate roof, the only one like it. Duncan saw her first, and turned to everybody, rubbing his chest, to show he had seen the big clasp or buckle that she fastened her shawl with, shining nearly like silver where the brass showed through. She was about the chief of them all in this place, and the island of Faransay was said to belong to her. She spoke some soft words to them all that Colin did not hear, and then went away up the strand again.

Alasdair, who limped down to the shore while she was

76

speaking, had something to say too. "I cannot go up and down now," he said. "But you will all go, and you will not all come back, but you all shall." No one could ask him what he meant, because he began to play 'The Keppoch Rade'.

The bag of the bagpipes went under his arm. It was how a man would carry a baby, Colin's mother said. Then, with Alasdair blowing in the mouthpiece (like blowing into the baby's leg) the bag began to grow, sticking out things like arms and the other leg, and beginning to moan. It is easy to understand what Mrs Henderson meant.

But there is no helping the noise before the tune. There are droning pipes the bag breathes out through that cannot be stopped, as well as the pipe with holes in, the chanter, that goes in the hands to play the tune.

Alasdair walked slowly along the edge of the water, and children ran beside him. Those going in the boat waded out and climbed aboard. Colin lifted in a wet Cathal, and climbed in himself. He sat up in the bow and rested against a tup's back. The tup now and then droned out his own sudden bleat under the other music, not liking Cathal so near.

Others came to give the boats a push away: the big one had touched the sand again. Anabel climbed among the people and would come close to Colin, but her mother made her sit further back and have her hair combed.

Colin did not think of her. He was busy now being in the boat, and feeling it move under him, thinking too that in his wallet he carried reeds for the time when he would be a piper, to walk the shore beside departing boats, or be next the fire at feasts.

The boat began to feel the slopes of the sea, to lift and lift again. The tups began to try to get up and get out. Duncan came up in the bow with Colin, to settle them, and to point the way the boat should be steered. The oars were lifted out and went into the water.

There was a big boat. Colin, Duncan, the tups, and a great many more, men, women, children and dogs, were in it. Tied to its side, at the stern, was a smaller boat, full of firewood first, with people on top. Both boats were made of sticks and leather, the hides of cows thickly coated with old fat, rancid and stinking. The top edge, or gunnel, round the boats was worn black and clean with being touched, and the panels between the wooden frames had long been rubbed dark; but close to the wood, and between the sinewy stitches joining the hides there lurked a pungent hairy wax that would not wash away from a hand that touched it. The best place to travel would have been on the raft of firewood trailing behind them, there being no wood to be got on the island. In both boats leak water had to be cupped up and put over the side.

Faransay was still only sun and shadow. The land they had left began to be the same, a lightly stained smudge between sea and sky. But still could be seen on the strand the walking shape of Alasdair, alone now that everyone else had gone home; still the sound of the pipes carried over the gentle air and quiet waves. Then they were no more and, even when the boat lifted a little, Alasdair could no longer be seen marching the place between land and water.

They went further and further from that misty shore. Faransay grew large and clearer to the right, and brighter and darker as the boat went round it. There was no beach on the landward side, and the boats had to come round to the seaward coast, where there seemed to be nothing for ever, except on the days that a ship sailed past between unknown ports.

They came round to the landing place slowly and quietly. They stopped before touching land, in a bay between rocks.

"We are visitors here," said Colin's father, quietly to quiet people. "It is well to remember we do not know who lives here. So before we are landed we will send the Gift. When we are landed we shall mind our manners, and take nothing but our own lambs. We are to be very harmless, because it is not only our manners we must mind, but our living."

78

3

"We have the Gift," said Mrs Tivert.

"Very well," said Colin's father.

"Anabel is to take it," said Mrs Tivert. Colin's father said nothing, meaning that no one should speak or move: silence and stillness were right at this time.

They sat under the high hill of the island, on the full, calm tide, with the breathing water slapping gently at the black rocks and stroking the narrow beach. Faransay was all sunshine and shadow. The smell of the heather came down like honey; sheep called from the upper distance; a gull signalled with wing and cry.

The boat rocked gently. In the middle of it women bent over Anabel, straightening, smoothing, tidying, rubbing with licked cloth, encouraging in whispers.

Duncan watched Anabel and Colin's father. When he had the sign he wanted he climbed out of the boat, the water to his waist. Someone whispered last things to Anabel, and handed her to Duncan, giving her a cloth bundle and a bowl to carry. The bowl had milk, the cloth had bannocks.

Duncan carried her towards the shore, and set her down in knee-deep water. The women in the boat hissed and clucked like geese and hens.

Anabel walked out of the water, then stopped to look

79

back. She was crying. The fuss made to encourage and help her had frightened her. Now she was further upset by a boat-load of people staring at her. The boat shook as all the women started to give signals that meant "Go on". Anabel went on, looked back once more, and turned off among the rocks and heather. She went out of sight. There was half a minute when no one breathed. This was the time, the women said, it was now, when the fairies of the island decided whether to accept the Gift or keep the child. They could do either. It was known they had kept Colin's father's mother's cousin, that Alasdair the piper had been going to wait for until she was grown. He was still waiting forty or more years later.

Anabel came back into sight without the bowl or the cloth. The women all breathed in, because they believed; the men breathed out because they did not. Duncan went to bring Anabel back. But still they had to wait. Something had yet to tell them whether it was time to leave the boat.

Duncan told them. He gave one of his shouts, but did not know. It was only the shout that meant he was impatient, and he would give it when his dinner was late or when he wanted someone to stop talking and come to work: it did not mean he had a message from the island. Colin's father looked at Colin, and his look meant "Say nothing", so Colin kept a firm mouth. His father started the rowing again. The boat came on to the beach and rubbed at it.

When he stepped on the island Colin found it was land like home. He thought it should have a looser feel to it: islands look as if they float.

Work began at once. It had taken half a morning to load up and get here, and the boats were to row back and forth between land and island the next days, loaded with lambs.

Colin was to go about the gathering of sheep with Duncan. "You will know what to do, you and Cathal," said his father, "but you do not know the ground. Duncan knows the ground. There is no hurry; bring them back gently."

The men set off round the island. The women began to make fires in cooking places, and build shelters.

There was not much to say to Duncan in their walking, and not much that he had to say either. Cathal started a hare, and they all wanted to run after it, but there was work to do. That had been on top of the hill, in a bare place they came to as they crossed the island. From the top they could see the water going on for ever at one side, and at the other the point of land where their own village was, far off the colour of a vein under the skin.

They came down from the hill-top to trees at the edge of huge cliffs, where the sea lay hundreds of feet down and the cliff cut the land away among the ash, rowan and elder. Far underfoot the sea sucked and brushed.

Cathal found something else among the black rocks on this high edge, dancing with excitement and shouting what he intended to do. Deep in a crack in the rocks something growled back, squalled, and spat like a musket. Duncan watched and sniffed, hearing nothing. He padded his fingers on his knee, and then clawed with them. He meant "Wild cat". Colin hauled Cathal away. In a fight the wild cat would win.

"You know that," he said to Cathal. "Come away." Cathal knew, and came away.

They walked along the cliff-top. Colin felt the depth pulling at him yards from the edge. He began to feel hungry. He mentioned it to Duncan in signs. Duncan looked at the sun, and it was not high enough yet.

They came on some sheep and sent them up the hill. Men walking round the shore of the island would start all the sheep in the right direction. At a place where the cliffs broke away into a gap, Duncan waited. He could not explain why. But soon Alan MacDonald came through the trees the other side of the gap with his black dog. When they had spoken to him they turned back and up the hill a little, further inland. They set the sheep on their way again.

It was all walking, and with Duncan there was not much conversation. For Colin, Duncan's thoughts stayed inside; for Duncan, Colin's thoughts did the same.

Duncan still did not think it was time to eat. Colin longed for the bannocks and milk Anabel had left among

81

the rocks of the shore, though they were a Gift he could not eat and perhaps ought not to think about. In the wallet slung at his side he could feel what he had with him. There was the hard bulge of a flint, the flat stiffness of a piece of knife blade, and the denseness of the tight tinder, all for striking fire. There was the leatheriness of oatcake, the roundness of a wedge of cheese, and the creaking springiness of a cabbage leaf that wrapped them. He thought of the bannock, not of them.

With them in the wallet were the dry stems of elder that he had cut that morning at Alasdair's house. He longed as well to take one, cut a tongue in it, and sound a note.

Then he found a curiosity. They were walking a path among bushes and rocks. Cathal was in front, and saw the thing like a twig in the path. He sniffed it, did not like it, and went on. Duncan went past without seeing it. But Colin saw it shine, like a made thing.

It was a short pipe, less than a foot long, swelled at one end, with white bands of fine bone round it, and tips of bright metal, like gold. Down it ran a row of holes.

It was the chanter of a set of pipes, like Alasdair's, but richer. Colin could not understand how Duncan had not seen it. He picked it up, rubbed the dark wood, and looked at it. If it needed a single reed he would be able to sound it; and of all those on the island Duncan was the one who would not hear.

Colin took his knife in one hand, the chanter in the other, and stepped off the path behind a rock. Duncan could not hear, but might see.

4

Colin knew what to do. He had seen Alasdair; he had been shown; he had done it for himself. "The chanter was there for me, perhaps," he said, "and I am meant to do it." But at the same time he knew that Duncan would not have approved, that Cathal would have been impatient.

He untied his wallet. He took out the food and laid it on a stone. He was not troubled with that hunger now; that could wait. The flint and tinder he did not disturb. He took into his hand one of the slips of elderwood.

He pulled off the thicker end of the chanter, the place where the reed fits into the bore. He put the slip of wood in the bore. It fitted like finger to glove. He cut the wood to the length of the mouthpiece.

He hollowed the twig next, taking out dry pith, letting it scatter to the ground. He began with the point of his knife and continued as Alasdair had, with a splinter from another length of elderwood.

When he had blown the last dust clear he made the tongue, cutting it along the side of the tube. He put the tube in his mouth, stopped the inner end with his tongue, and breathed out. A muted note buzzed in his head. He thought no one heard.

He put the reed aside while he looked for something to stop the end with. The breath does not blow through the reed, but through the tongue and then through the pipe of the instrument. At last he pasted oatcake and cheese together with a little spit, and used that.

He put the mouthpiece on the chanter, over the reed. It was time to play; but first he wrapped up his wallet and came back to the sheep-path he and Duncan had been following.

The tune came to him in some way he did not know, eight or ten notes leaping out from under his fingers, plain and dry at first, then alive when he put in the shakes that separate the notes. He played it among the trees as he walked the path.

Cathal heard and came running back, barking. Duncan was in sight, across a clearing, down a glade, towards the edge of the trees. Colin put the pipe away in the wallet and walked on to join him. He did not show him the fine thing he had found; dark wood, ivory, and gold.

Duncan indicated that they would go on as they were for not much longer, then turn and meet Alan MacDonald and eat with him. Colin saw that the time for food would come, and could wait, though his hunger had come back greatly.

However, in a very little while his mouth filled with water, not because of the food he expected, but because he smelt food he did not expect. He smelt the most delightful food there could be. He was not able to decide exactly what it was, but there was roasted meat to it, with onion and some rich herb; there was the coddling of apples, and the smoking of herring; there was the brewing of beer and the grinding of coffee; there was the stewing of beef and the toasting of cheese; there was the churning of butter and the scalding of cream; there was the baking of bread and the frying of chops; there was the spitting of pigs and the charring of chestnuts; there was the boiling of pudding and the foaming of wine.

It was nothing like oatcake, pulpy cheese, and a cabbage leaf. His belly twitched, rumbled, and felt a pain of hunger.

Duncan smelt nothing. Cathal smelt something not food. Colin did not think of foods he could name, but the meaning and intent of them came into his mind.

84

Duncan went on walking. Colin stopped. He had to find where the smell came from. Over to the right, on the inland side, the trees grew thinner and there was open ground. He went that way, and the smell grew stronger. He came out of the trees into the sunshine, with Cathal following him. Cathal's back ruffed up, but Colin only thought of hedgehogs, baked, not of danger.

There was a little house of turf in the open place, with light at it. It seemed a brighter place than the sunshine. It was the place to go to, but it was not easy to get there: it seemed to get smaller as Colin approached. But the smell of food grew stronger: pies and pastry, strawberry and cinnamon, cake and honey.

He wondered about Duncan for a moment, knowing that he must catch up now and not be loitering here. In that moment he found himself at the door of the little bothy, thinking it was like home, and like more than home. And while he thought and knew he should not be here, or do it, he stepped over the doorstone.

For another moment he was alone. Cathal stayed outside, puzzled. Colin was at once in the middle of the place, the centre of a bright, high room, larger by far than the bothy it was in. Cathal was not to be seen. Colin was not alone now. The room was full of people, so full and so moving with them that he could not tell who they were. There were more people here than he knew, but he felt he knew them all, each one. But no sooner had he recognized one than another came in front, to be known afresh. It was puzzling, and made him dizzy. Was that Mrs MacDonald, with the golden buckle? Was that Alasdair, with the pipes? Did Duncan walk beyond that table? Could he see Mrs Tivert and Anabel?

And was it a dance that went on? Or a feast? Or was it marching, or a great council? It was hard to tell, or there was no way to be sure. Only the sme l of food was strong in his head.

"Welcome, Colin," someone said. Was it Mrs Tivert? Or Mrs MacDonald from the slate-roofed house?

"Where is this place?" said Colin, and it was like talking to no one at all, as if the person spoken to had gone quietly out of the door before he had begun his words.

"This is what we give you all," said the person. "This is what we give you, all that come here. Sit at the table and eat, Colin, eat our sweet roast lamb."

And there he was, sitting at a thick table, and a dish in front of him held lamb broken from the roast, steaming, juicy, pink, soft.

"We are all here," said another, Alasdair perhaps. "Eat; welcome."

Colin took up a fragment of the meat and put it to his mouth. As his teeth closed down upon it he knew it was wrong. When the meat came into his mouth it changed. It was meat no longer. It was not worse than meat, but it was no more than good plain bannock. Before he could decide clearly about the wrongness, he had chewed and swallowed, and before he thought again he had lifted his hand that held now a beaker of bubbling red wine and put it to his lips, and drunk, but drank milk.

He knew then, with sudden shock, that he had eaten and drunk the offering, the Gift; he knew that this was the house of the fairies, and that he should not have come, should not have bitten or sipped. He saw that he was in an empty place indeed, like a dismal cave with a dirty sky for roof; that there were few folk there and none he knew; and that there were no doors out.

"Play the pipe for us once and then go," said one of them. "It is not much to ask."

For a moment there was a sound stronger than the voices close round Colin, not louder, but more real. It was the voice of Duncan calling his name time after time, coming near and then going far, and then gone. It was not possible, for Duncan had no voice to say words he could not hear, yet it had been Duncan calling.

"Dance with us," said one of the people of the place. There were few of them now, and they were real. The speaker was to him like Mrs MacDonald, without seeming like her at all. And then, when Colin thought of Alasdair, Alasdair was whom he almost saw and nearly heard.

These were the people of the island, the race of fairies. "Play for us," said another of them. Colin did not believe in them, but they did not go away.

"Then leave," said another. Their hands were picking and plucking at his sleeve and his wallet. Colin was trying to call to Duncan and answer him, but with the taste of bannock and milk in his mouth, staining his throat, he could not open one or use the other. As he stood there, something seemed to be running from his heart. It was like forgetting who he was, his life and how he had been brought up and what he had ever done. Or perhaps all that he knew about the world and himself was getting further and further away, smaller and smaller.

In the few minutes that the fairy people were pestering him to play he had become used to them, and used to where he was. He forgot he did not believe in them.

He had recovered from the shock of knowing he had eaten what he should not. He felt at home even though he saw that the people were not any he knew, but their own small selves. He could see that they were harmless and a little sad, and in a sorry place. Up in their wan white sky there was no sun; down here there would be no fire, no hot, no cold.

"A tune, a tune," they were saying.

"I will play you a dance," he said, and it seemed to him that he had shouted, and it seemed to them the same, because they turned about, leaned away, and covered their ears. "I will play," he said, very gentle, very quiet. Now he could speak, but it was of no use to call Duncan, and there was no time. He had to think what tune he could play. While he thought the people ran about the place clearing the floor of tables and benches and dishes, all in a great confusion. Where one band had cleared a space another would put tables, rugs, goblets, thrones, and others would wheel across a cart and put that in the middle of the dancers who had begun before the music. Fairy horses and their riders came pawing in and stood where they could, where dancing space had been cleared.

"Play, play," they shouted, while some heaved boulders across the dance floor, and some brought in the strange stem of a grassy tree and left it where it must be hopped over. But they were so graceful that obstacles did not matter.

He took the chanter from his wallet, put it against his mouth, and blew gently. All the tune he knew was what had come to him as he walked the path under the trees, going towards Cathal and Duncan.

He thought he played it once only. Something happened to the tune and the time and the dance, and they went on faster and faster, higher and higher, wilder and wilder, until there was a sudden end, like the echo of a bang. All the people poured away out of sight, taking their goods with them, leaving Colin alone.

88

He thought he would go home now. He had played to them, and he expected they would keep their word. He looked to see what the place was like now they were out of it.

He was sitting on a rock close by some small trees. The light in the sky had gone, and he saw by the light of a moving glow that travelled up into the air, went over in a bow, and down to the ground, which it dipped under leaving darkness; and sudden cold clapped down on him, and moving things bumped in the night. The glow looped up again out of the ground, made a day, and then night again. During the next loop he ran to it as it came to the ground and caught hold, to avoid another night, like catching the sun.

It burst in his hand. He was holding a rushlight, or taper, that varied in weight, heavy at first as it remembered going down, then less so, as it remembered going up.

There was a path. It seemed untrodden, but clearly there. He went along it among trees. The trees were stiff and still: like the path, they seemed to have been made but never used. The path ran out. It was no longer ahead of him, and when he turned it was not behind him either, as if it had dried up. He thought he had come nowhere, because he was standing against the rock where he had begun.

Now the taper in his hand grew too light and too heavy, more than he could hold. But he did hold it longer, while it wrenched at his hands, and his arms, and then his whole body, wresting itself away.

He was not alone. There was another rock not far from where he sat, like the other cheek of a gateway. On it sat a girl a little older than himself, but not much. She looked at him. He looked at her. He thought she was very ugly indeed, so broad and clumsy, so wide a face and such coarse hair, and an unhandsome colour, with pale eyes that glared hollow. He thought her so blotched and lumpish that he did not like to look.

Then the tugging taper hauled him off the rock, and brought him nearer to her. They looked at one another.

She opened her mouth, and what great teeth she had, and a tongue like a calf.

The taper lifted beyond the amount he could hold it, and soared up above them, hung there as he looked at the girl, and then descended.

By the time it reached the ground Colin had looked at her enough. He turned and walked away. He did not go far before darkness and cold fell upon him. But he went on walking through those minutes of night, and through the next rising of day, and into the next night.

In that darkness he fell over his own feet and hurt both legs, bruising and banging them on stones. He stayed where he was until light came again, then looked to see what he had done.

He did not know what he was seeing. His own hands were so ill-formed, so hideous; his own legs were so badly different from his idea of what they should be like, his skin so marked and hairy, that he thought he must be changed. But then he knew he was comparing his own real self with the fairy people so thin and fine. He had not changed, only his idea of things had altered.

He felt a deep shame at walking away from a girl of his own kind, no more ugly and awkward than himself. Through a loop of day and one of night he sat, and then he turned about and went to her. He took her hand, and it was smaller than his.

"Will you fetch me home?" she said. "They will be looking."

6

Colin was certain he had come back to the girl with nothing but thoughts about helping her. But when she spoke and asked him for help he knew that he had truly come to her for it, to be looked after. When he realized that he felt he was bound to fail her. He let go of her hand. He saw that his own hand was big and ugly, and that hers was small and ugly. There was nothing to choose between them: the fairy people were beautiful beyond measure; people like himself and the girl were gross. She looked at his face.

"Are you a goblin?" she asked. "You look like one."

"I am Colin," he said. "We have to go out of here."

"Yes, take me home," she said. "I have forgotten the way."

"Duncan will be looking for me," said Colin. He wanted Duncan to come up and find him now; he wanted Cathal to be near and real, touching him with a wet nose, smelling of dog.

"It will be trouble," said the girl. "Perhaps I shall get back before they miss me. It is not long since I had my dinner here. I have not yet finished. I thought I would finish first, but I am weary and all the people have gone." And she lifted up from her lap a barley bannock, just like all those that Colin had ever seen, flat below and rounded

91

over, smoothed and browned from the bake-stone.

"I must finish it and then go home," she said. "I would be beside my mother's hearth if I could."

"What is your name?" he said. "And where are you from?"

"My name is Janet," she said. "I live at my mother's, and where else would I?"

"Well, I will take you out of here," said Colin, thinking that if he spoke and decided then matters might come right. When his father spoke firmly things became right; but that might be for other reasons than saying so. "You will not be needing the bannock. It is not far, Janet."

So she jumped clump down from the rock, and the bannock tumbled down from her knee beside it, and rolled away.

"Leave it," said Colin. She too had eaten fairy food, he saw.

"Then which way are we going?" she asked.

Colin was wondering that already. There was nothing here to tell him which way led out into the woods. If Duncan would call again that would guide him; he had seemed to hear him once, yet Duncan could not have called any name, and did not know shouting.

It was of no use to show doubt or hesitation. He looked round, like Duncan seeing the weather. Over to one side the looping glow of light rose and fell, bright and dark. It was moving further away. It took its light away with it, and it took its own patch of dark with it too. Now round Colin and Janet there was the grey twilight he had thought so bright when he approached the bothy.

"If we walk," he said, "we shall come to the edge of the island. If we follow the little winding paths we shall get lost, so we shall go in a straight line."

They walked away from the rocks they had sat on, and Colin set a direction.

The ground here was something like a shadow. It was firm enough to walk on, but not firm enough to be seen. The trees, and rocks, and stiff flowering things that grew, went into shadow before reaching earth. It was like walking in muddy but completely dry water. Colin could see his own ungainly feet below him, but Janet's, a little way off, were not visible.

Overhead the sky was full of dark bruises, and in each one shone a faint light: they were the stars of the place, each with its darkness round it. Now and then in their walking, they came to a tree, or passed a clump of nettles, or docks, or rushes. Nothing moved but themselves. Colin began to wonder if a path might not have been better: he did not know whether he wondered because he saw, or saw because he wondered: a little to one side there lay a firm grassy path, smooth and inviting. Janet wanted to be on it, but Colin thought it was too good to be true. Though it looked as if it led where they wanted to go, he could not be sure.

"We shall stick to our way," he said. Then the path, or another one, lay across their way. "Straight on," he said. He stepped over without touching, but Janet put her foot on it as she crossed.

"Oh listen," she said. Colin stepped back to her, and his heel stood on the edge of the green grass. All at once, and for a moment only, birds sang, warmth came in the air, and colour over the whole surrounding view, there was the smell of fresh earth and heather, and a feeling of comfort. It came to him like a flash of lightning, and went away. Something had stroked his mind with delight. But his heel came off the path, and he was back in grey gloom.

Janet had left the path too. "Did you feel it?" she asked. "Did you hear? It was the great court again, and I was nearly the queen at it."

"There was something," said Colin. But he did not trust it to be real; and he knew they had experienced different things.

"Go back," said Janet. But when they turned to look, the path crossing their way had disappeared. "Oh, oh," she said and she had tears on her face, "if I am there it is all I ever want, but now I am here I want to be at home, and I can do neither, and it is dreadful to be only with you." So she wept a little, and then stopped.

It is only a girl, Colin thought, even if it is older. I shall

93

have to manage it all. "I am sure this is the way to go home," he said. "We must go on."

They followed a valley that opened up into a hollow place with grey grass in it, grey rock, and a grey furry distance, land and sky all one without a join.

Down in the bottom of this hollow there was a place where water might be, bare patches in the grass where there was nothing but dusty rock.

One or two of the places held a strange luminosity, as if they had water in them, water that must not only reflect sky; light must be refracted through. Colin put his head over one and felt light strike him, and saw his own lit face looking back at him. He was putting down a hand to touch the water when he saw something more. Round his reflected hand there was a spreading shadow of dark that became a transparency of the surface, so that he saw a fire burning beyond, with women cooking, and his father seeing back at him; but when he tried to go through, the women ran, his father stretched out a hand, and the water dried to rock.

"These places are footprints," said Janet. She saw neither water here, nor other places beyond.

7

"Are you to kneel there all day?" said Janet. "What is it with you?"

"It is nothing," said Colin. But he had knelt after the vision of his father in the shining speculum had dried to dust; he had knelt feeling that half of himself had been torn out and gone home. He felt more than he knew he could. It was as if he had not been home for a year. But he had to leave thinking of it when Janet spoke.

"It is like a long day," he said, "or a long time of day."

It felt as if Duncan, and Alan with his black dog, would at this moment be taking their meal together at the meeting place. When he thought that he felt guilty about playing the chanter, because to do so was not forthrightly bravely honest. But at the same time he felt he had been right to do it, although it was more than Duncan could understand. That is how the world is, too plain for others to see.

The chanter was in his wallet. He got it out, laid his fingers on the eight holes, and breathed through it.

"What is that?" said Janet as he lifted it to his lips. "You are to be taking me on my way."

Colin breathed. The reed sounded.

When it spoke, like the cry of a bird, there settled on him a warm pleasure, round him the grey ground drew back,

95

and in its place there glowed out in sudden colour a lawn of grass and flowers, a patch of brightness in which both of them sat. When he played another note a tree sprang up; when the tune he knew and had made flowed out, the place it created flew with birds; a burn ran silvery beside them; the flowers in the grass stood tall; and butterflies of unknown vivid colours settled there, unrolling long trunks to take nectar; the sky filled blue; sunshine dropped light on them and shadows behind them.

The tune ended. There was no way to delay that end, and at it the colours faded, the butterflies departed, the water dried, the sky dimmed, the tree dissolved to mist, the grass was flooded with the indistinct grey of the desolate valley they were in, and there was nothing. He played another note, but there was still nothing, and he knew it would be so.

"We must go on walking," he said. "It is like a sea-fog. We can see further, but there is nothing in sight. In fog follow the water down."

"That is so," said Janet. "We shall reach the sea, or Loch Dove, and it is not many miles home."

That was so; Colin would have said it himself. It was a thought they were both comforted by. Perhaps because they felt happy and refreshed after Colin's tune, they lingered where they were.

Then, when they moved down the valley, it was not long before they came again on a path crossing their way.

"Do not step on it," said Colin. It was a hard thing to say, because this path was too wide to step over. "We shall walk and not stop," he said. "It is not a right place we have got into, and that part of it is less right again." And he strode on, taking Janet's hand.

Almost at once she pulled away from him. Colin had been ready for a change in everything, because it had happened before. But he had not expected to be so strongly in the middle of a great rout and run of the beautiful fairy people, laughing, shouting and full of delight to see him again. Janet had gone.

He went after her, with the people calling to him, asking for a tune, plucking at his clothes, and confusing everything that he did, so that he forgot time after time what he was doing (looking for Janet), and why (to get her and himself home).

He became so surrounded he could not move. The fairy people are delicate and without weight, but in many hundreds they become like snow without the cold, too deep for walking.

He had to play them a tune, It was the best thing he could do, because it made them move, and when they were dancing to each other he could move among them.

Janet was not moving. He saw her picking something from the floor of the dancing place, and came to her. She was taking up the bannock she had left long before, because they were in that place again and the people had offered it to her.

Then a darkness came through the throng. "Play, play," said the fairies. "It is the moon."

And the moon came by. Earlier Colin had caught the sun, at the same point, coming in its darkness, rising from the ground and looping up then dipping into it again. The moon came in her darkness, a changing and a milder light as it spun, looping up and over, the fairies scattering out of the darkness, but filling its light with a throb and flutter and spinning dizziness.

In one hand Janet held the bannock. In the other she would catch the moon, as Colin had caught the sun. But the moon would not wait, and passed by, leaving Colin and her for a moment in the darkness the fairy people shunned.

In that darkness there was only the grey of the outer floor of this world, only the distances of nothing.

"I used to play with a ball," Janet was saying, but she was in the light of the dance, and Colin was in the grey other place, in the valley leading to the sea or the loch, and home. "Indeed I was this morning only, before I took that bad dinner."

"Away from there now," said Colin, and when he stopped playing to speak the dance stopped too. He pulled Janet into the darkness with him, and they stood in the twilight, and melting before them the fairies turned their faces to Colin. But that sight all narrowed to a green path across the ground, the voices and presence died down into it, and the path itself was no more.

"We are through that," said Colin.

"It is my bannock back again," said Janet.

"Throw it down," said Colin. "It will make you stay too."

"I am not sure I will go home," said Janet.

"It is just down the valley," said Colin. "It is where I am going."

They went on. Janet still carried the bannock. Colin began to remember his own dinner in his wallet, seeing it as he put away the chanter.

The valley did not lead to the sea, though they thought for a moment that it had. It led to a wall of rock with a great crack down it. When they came close Colin saw the sea beyond the gap. It seemed to him that they were in the deep of the narrow crack, and that the sea was outside and beyond, blowing light towards them.

But it was another of the sights of the home world. Janet saw it too. When they stood against the lip of the crack they saw the sea rising and falling, with a boat in it full of people. Colin could not pick out a face, but Janet called, and the vision went.

"Oh," she said, "it was my mother. I thought of her outwith my head."

But they were outside a dark passage in rock, going in, not inside coming out; and that was the only way to go.

8

The song of the sea they had seen, the memory of people left behind and waiting for them, the feel of the boat heaved up and down by the water, were with Colin. He had known them all not long ago. Day and night had not changed since he came to this place on the island, but something had gone astray with time.

"Are we to go in?" said Janet.

"If we go back up the valley we do not come to the edge of the island," said Colin. "I think we are to go on. Water goes to water, to the sea or to the loch."

They stepped inside the crack.

"There will be spiders," said Janet.

Colin looked up the sides of the narrow place they were in, vertical and gently curving and rounding, smooth to a high edge with the grey sky beyond. Light came down the chasm almost to their feet. It was as if dusk had fallen to the bottom and was to be waded through.

Colin led the way. Janet took a fim grip of the back of his clothes. There was no room to walk abreast.

They went along a level floor, with some small stones to stumble on. The way began to turn and twist, sometimes becoming so narrow that the ground vanished, and they were climbing up the sides of the cleft, clambering on the rock itself.

"It doesn't lead anywhere," said Janet.

"If it doesn't we shall come back," said Colin. "Hush you." He was trying to think how time had gone. They had spent time being in this fairy part of Faransay, and that time felt as if it had been, and as if it had not. He considered that the best part of a day might have passed. But time less than a day was not important to him. Mrs MacDonald had a clock in her house, standing up and drumming to itself, and now and then singing out. Colin could not see what it did that was not happening without it. Even when it had stopped, and been talked about, all the week had gone by in the usual way. What can be smaller than a day? he wondered. But for now, whatever the time was doing, he had to plod along.

Then there was water splashing on him, as he went from foot to foot. When he had the lifted foot down on the ground again he was in a howling sudden gale of rain and hail, the wind making him deaf and dizzy, a wind out of nowhere, immediate, strong, and cold. Behind the wailing of the wind was the rage of the sea, and up out of the ground, it seemed, there came a wave, breaking on his feet and drawing at them as it sank down again.

As well as the fury of storm there was the blinding brilliance of painful light. So he stood and sheltered his body with his arms and his face with his hands and tried to hold the ground with his feet, while he staggered and his wits were scattered.

He was standing firmly within a few seconds, about to take the breath that had been snatched from him, when Janet pushed him aside and came past. They were out of the cleft in the rock now, and on a ledge overlooking the sea, overlooking it from a great height; and it was a strong storm to blow and drive the waves up the cliff as high as the ledge and higher.

Colin thought she would stand with him, and he put out an arm to hold her. She pushed beyond that, and before he knew what to do she had jumped from the edge and gone from sight.

He thought she called out as she went, but it was not in words. Then she seemed to call louder and louder, in more than one voice. He understood that she was among people.

He followed her to the edge, and had to kneel and crawl to get there. He saw, far below, the writhing, rising sea, sending its heads of foam up the huge cliff, lifting, falling, biting at the land.

A little below, looking up and down and from side to side, was Janet, on a step of the cliff, near enough to reach.

"They were all here," she shouted. "It was my fireside and this was the hearthstone."

Colin reached down his hand, pulling her up to where he was. They both crouched while the wind hit and the rain stung.

"I could hear them," said Janet. Colin could hear them too.

They heard the voices of birds. The birds came flying out of the storm at them; gulls, gannets, fulmars, and hooked eagles, swooping down the current of wind, or reining up against it and hanging at their faces; diving down the higher cliff, or lifting up it on a rising draught; coming a yard clear, a foot near, an inch sheer, until Colin and Janet backed away from the edge and looked for the place they had come from, to go back into the crack and retrace their steps.

There was no cleft in the rock. The cliff was solid when they came to it. They had to move to right or left along the ledge. When they went right the birds attacked more closely, slapping with great busy wings, the hot fishy oil of the fulmars in their nostrils, the decaying dust of the eagles in their mouths.

They turned to go left. As they went, step by step, the birds stopped flying at them. They seemed also to become smaller, as if they had moved away about a mile. They glittered black and white, and scurried harmlessly about Janet's head. Colin brushed them away. They began to settle on him, changed to a silent soft snow.

Colin and Janet went along the ledge into a sheltered bay, high over the water. They were warm when the battering wind stopped blowing on them.

They looked out to sea. They were on the edge of the island; there was no doubt of that, with home in sight:

miles away across the wild water lay the outline of the hills standing above the village. But there was no way from one to the other.

"We came to the water's edge," said Colin. "But too high up."

"I thought I was home," said Janet. "It is dreadful not to be. I should not have done it. I should not."

"What was it you did?" said Colin.

"I ate the Gift," said Janet. "I was hungry and I ate the Gift as I gave it. I wish they will let me go soon, but these people do not know about soon: it is all the same to them, and my mother will be looking."

Well, thought Colin, this is not Anabel Tivert, so I do not understand. But she must not eat again, or they will have her.

He saw that from here they could escape only by climbing the cliff. Above them it was sloping, broken, not steep. They set out towards it. On the way they had to cross a running burn, and in the middle there was a bright pool. Both saw it and both looked. Colin saw through at once, to where himself sat by the hearth at home, with a knife and stick, and where his mother looked full at him over her knitting needles, looked and stayed a stitch. Then Janet dipped a hand in the water, and the picture went.

9

The birds had gone, settled to snow, or blizzarded away to sea. Colin had begun to feel comfortable about one thing. He was sure they had come out into his own sort of world, and were no longer in the strange fancies of the fairy lands.

"It was not canny about the birds," he said. "That is all."

"We shall get away down to the water," said Janet. "Yes, indeed we shall."

Comforted and escaped were two sensible things to think, now they were climbing the broken cliff. Their heads felt clearer; they could see their own world; the cliff itself was real, with no shadow at their feet, no grey twilight. The light though dim, with shifting clouds overhead, was true daylight.

But watchers were there. A slaty shell of rock came skittering down the boulders between Colin and Janet. Janet looked down to see where it went. Colin looked up to see where it came from, because gone is gone, but to come can be avoided. And something, he thought, had dislodged it.

There was another stone coming, falling through the air towards him. As he saw that it would go to one side and not hit either of them, he felt the world of the fairies creeping back round him. He resisted, pushing it from him, but he could not hold it off or break through. It was like being taken in an invisible net that altered the way things were seen, holding him back as well without seeming to be there.

The stone went wide, bounced on a rock, thudded further down the cliff, and landed dully in shadow. It was the shadow that had covered the ground, and it had come again, and with it the twilight. Across the sea a grey mist settled, and the real world went out of sight. But there was one gleam, along the cliff, that might be sunlight.

The watchers stayed. They were part of the land. They were not the dancing people. In fact it was not clear whether they were people at all. Colin thought they were, but when he looked he considered they might be foxes, or wildcats. One of them he saw come down and sit on a rock, like a dwarf or monkey, looking away from him. He was able to creep up to it and touch it. His eyes had never left it, but it was grass when he held it. He thought he could not have watched steadily, yet as he held the grass it turned to dust, trickled out of his fingers down the rock, and slithered away like a pine-marten in the woods, a shape moved and gone before it is seen.

They worked over towards the gleam, hoping it was the true light of the sun.

It was a mysterious waterfall, running thin and fast down a smooth face of cliff, the light not shining on it, but from a thousand little shifting pictures that lay in the tumbling ripples, each one showing and changing its scene. Colin saw himself, his home, Cathal, alive, moving, going, dazzling. Janet saw many things.

"It is when I was a bairn," she said, "see, there, and here is my mother, and that is a piper lad, and our red cow."

The water was thin as skin, and when the light went it was a wet black rock, nothing more, drying to the smoky mist that covered this world.

They came all at once to the top of the cliff.

"We have been to the edge," said Janet angrily. "There is nothing next, is there? How are you to be at another edge from this one? What is the way? We are having a full time going nowhere."

104

"It is my fault I am here," said Colin. "But it is not my fault that you are here. So do not scold me."

But she had spoken like that because she was unhappy again, and sick for home. She began to sniff and sob.

"And do not greet," said Colin, crossly. But that did not stop her. It seemed to him that she was older and ought to be able to manage better than he could, so why should he be in charge, when he was just as sick for home, just as lost? They sat down where they were, and each put a desperate arm about the other, and had a long cry.

When it was over their noses ran and their faces hurt. They sat where they were for a long time. Colin thought he could hear the sea, and when he had thought that he was strong enough to move again.

Perhaps they needed something to eat, since time must have passed beyond eating. He got out his wallet, and unwrapped the cabbage leaf and the oatcake and cheese.

It would not be eaten. He did not want it; there was no hunger in him. Janet said she would eat the bannock. Colin knew she had not brought it with her, but when she spoke of it there it was at her hand.

"It is getting smaller," she said. "I am not eating it, but it is getting less. It is down to a spindle weight now."

"I think you should not eat it at all," said Colin. "We should take nothing here that we have not brought in."

"I brought this," said Janet. "But it was given to the people of the island. Well, I stole it. But they can let me go home now; my mother will be waiting."

After this meal that they did not eat, Colin wrapping up the wallet again, and Janet dropping the bannock, they stood up and prepared to walk once more.

"We shall walk in a straight line," said Colin. "As much away from here as we can."

It was easy to say, and simple to begin. It was too simple.

"It is getting a path on its own," said Janet soon, because the grey mist at their feet had begun to form a straight way ahead of them.

"I do not like it," said Colin. "But it is the way we are going."

They followed the path. Soon they began to see a

considerable way ahead. The air grew brighter, and there came some colour in the tufts of vegetation they came across, a slight yellow of flowers, a touch of red on a seed case, and a blue hill far off. The way became more pleasant, and all round them became like a field, greening from below. They knew they had been led to a fairy dancing ground again when the path turned to a grassy one, and the landscape to the dancing floor, with the crowd all round them again asking Colin to play for a dance.

Colin ran from side to side, but could not get out of the place. He gave in then and brought out his chanter. Was it all, he wondered, from using the good-luck elder bough hung above the hearth?

"I will dance too," said Janet. "It is a lovely place to be in." Colin looked at her, and himself, and thought how thick and heavy they looked against the fairies, and how pale Janet's eyes were, more unreal than those of the fairies. The reason was that Janet's eyes were blue, and the fairies' eyes brown.

He played, not only the tune he knew already, but another part of it that came to him, and he knew it was the second quarter of his own music, that a piper should have, or what has he done for the music?

Around him the dance went on, as if it had always done so, and would do so, day after day, and night after night. With it Janet went, laughing, content, not heeding offers of bannock from the people. Then the fairy sun came through in its darkness, and when it did he and Janet stepped aside, though she did not want to, and they were once more at the two rocks where they had met.

106

10

"We are back again at the beginning," said Janet, sitting on the rock where Colin had first found her. "I can tell you, we shall be found dead in a day or two."

"That sort of day does not happen here," said Colin. But he sat on his rock and wondered whether they were ever to get back at all. For ever and for ever perhaps they would return here. But he did not say that to Janet. There was another way of looking at things. If these rocks were the middle of the island, which seemed likely, then they were half way across it again, half way to another side. They knew it too, and knowing was a blessing, if you can agree to know.

He tried to explain to Janet.

"Havers," she said. As far as she was concerned she had been put back where she started, and that was that. She had no hope, and Colin was talking nonsense.

"We'll take another turn," said Colin.

"We have done that," said Janet. "We have been to the water and we did not get to that. Too high, Colin."

"That was the sea," said Colin. "There is sea all round the island; it makes it so."

"Then away and find it," said Janet. "And if you come back for me I shall be here, but of course I shall be dead, and so shall you." She turned away and looked in another

107

direction; but she could still see him from the corner of her eye.

"Very well, I shall go," said Colin, after he had watched her and thought what he should do. Janet tightened her mouth and her throat, swallowed, and did not turn her head.

Colin looked a little longer, then walked off. He knew which way they had gone before, and went in the opposite direction.

He walked a hundred paces, and looked back. Janet had not moved. He walked ten more, and looked. Janet had not moved. He had thought she would follow, but she did not stir.

He took twenty paces more, and looked again. This time she was moving; her arms only, not getting from the rock to come after him. She turned her head. He saw her raising her hand to her mouth, and pushing back her hair.

He knew what she was doing. She was eating bannock. He turned fully and ran towards her. He knew she must not bite at what she had in her hand, because that would hold her for ever.

When he came close, those few seconds after he began running, he saw that she had been watching him and had not eaten.

"You are not to do that," he said, all in his tumbling breath. "No."

She stood up, looked squarely at him, lifted the diminished bannock, and put it to her mouth.

Colin jumped forward and pulled her hand from her mouth, taking the bannock away. She hit his ear with her other hand. She stamped on him with her foot. She bunched him with her knee. He tried to hold her, and stop her from eating. It was not enough. He had to shout at her and make her listen. She shouted and screamed back, and went on kicking sideways at him like a cow. Colin became cross, because she fought back when he was trying to help her. He shook her. They both shouted louder and louder, and the fighting began.

Colin did not want to fight at all; before he had begun he felt he had fought enough, because he had won what he wanted. Also, it is not easy to fight those who do not know the fashion of it.

She would not stop. "I will kill you," she said. But she had got down from screaming to speaking.

"No you will not," said Colin. "Now you will come with me and go where I go."

"Never will I do that," she said. By now she was not fighting hard, yet she was not giving in.

"You will come on," he said. He began to drag her the way he wanted to go. She tried to stand where she was, but he made her come a little way, having to walk backwards and haul her after him.

All at once she began to come more easily, and then she was pushing, and the fight had turned into a game and was all over.

"Will you come now?" said Colin.

She would not answer, but went on pushing and laughing. I have lost the fight, thought Colin; she has not given in, but never mind.

Yet he was a winner too, holding the bannock, small now like a coin in his hand. He put it in his wallet, against the oatcake. They went their way, hand in hand, quite happy.

They did not look where they were going. Together they stepped on a green path, and they were with the fairy people again, on the dancing floor. This time there was no crowd round them, no one asking for a dance. Something else was taking place.

On a raised-up place stood two chairs, or better than chairs, thrones. On the thrones sat the two important people of the fairies, crowned golden, silver buckled, with all the others looking towards them, talking, singing, listening, but most of all looking: that was enough, to look at their King and Queen, and King and Queen looking back, enough for them. It seemed that they were fed by looking at one another, and could not need anything else.

It was not easy to understand. Colin and Janet felt it too, and looked with the rest, not wanting to do any other thing for ever. The King and Queen were everything they could want or love or desire; with them nothing else would be needed.

How long they stood it was not possible to tell. They felt as if they had always been there. Then across them came the darkness of the rising, falling, moon of that place, spinning and glittering bleakly. And when the darkness had gone they were alone, though together, and out of the gathering of fairies.

They were back in the grey twilight, on the puffy ground again, and a little way ahead there was a change. A long shadow and a redness lay across the land. Beyond the shadow and the light lay a different sort of place.

"It is the sea again," said Colin. And it was the sea, when they came to it, as still and level as a mirror, against a white sanded beach, and with cliffed islands in it.

The water was so still that their own selves were reflected from it. It was so bright that light shone through from the world they knew.

Colin saw himself looking back, staring as he knew he was, but it was not reflection. Janet said, "Why, there is the piper lad, but he is dressed old. I do not understand why he looks it too." Colin's reflection turned away from him.

Then there was a shuffling rattle, and from a white cliff on another island slid a lip of rock into the sea, rippling its surface red, silver, and black; silver from itself, black from night hanging at one side of the sky, and red from a huge half sun at the other horizon.

"We are dead," said Janet.

"Yes," said Colin.

And they were both frightened at being so.

11

"These people will all die at once," said Janet. "Every one; they do not have souls like us, and that will be the end of them. But with us only the people that are alive can die, and all the dead ones are in heaven already. These people do not have that. I think this place is all there is, and that they have died, and we have because we are here, and we can't get to heaven."

"You are a strange girl," said Colin. "It is a bad place, no doubt, but we walked in and we can walk away."

The world in a bubble or drop of dew is sharp and curved. Being here was like being outside the bubble looking in, as well as being inside, part of the curving flatness, the sea sloping away to the edges of what could be seen, the sky a tight curve overhead, the beach of white sand being a bay and at the same time sloping back, the white rocks in the shining water tilted away yet showing their tops.

How they should get away was not clear. The beach was not an island, but the sea stretched ahead of them wherever they looked.

The sea flattened again, after its show of ripples. Slowly the sound of the ripples came to Colin's ears, one at a time, a pulsing beat made of the onset of many grains of sand, followed by a tail of fewer and fewer; it was as much a hiss as a rattle.

Colin still had the chanter in his hand, because he had got it out when they came among the fairy people, but had not been asked for a tune. The tune was ready to be heard, however. He began at the beginning, with what he played in the path behind Duncan, and then the second part from the dance, and then a third and most sad part, from this place, and still the tune was not ended. The words of the first part were, 'Under the sky, over the water', and of the second part, 'Small smoke from little fires', and the third, 'in my bed by the hearth yonder', and that was all he knew. There was more to come.

He would have played again, but no sound came when he tried.

"It is better with a tune," said Janet. "Go on again."

"The reed is broken," said Colin, "I believe. I shall make another in a while."

"Give it to me," said Janet. "I shall make it sound."

"No indeed," said Colin, holding the chanter away from her. "You cannot touch that."

"I do not know why," said Janet. "I am wanting the tunes more than you, and I brought nothing here to make them with."

"All the same, you are not having it."

"But perhaps it would bring all those people round us again," said Janet. "I am ashamed that I thought I could be queen at those places. Little girls only feel like that. That queen they gave is the lovemost person there ever was."

"And the king," said Colin, "I wish he would be among us all the time. Well there, I will try a tune again." He blew again, and there was nothing. "It is the reed," he said, and began to put the pipe away.

"I could be trying," said Janet. But Colin knew that would be wrong.

The white sand shimmered round them, like salt shaken on a plate, the grains leaping and falling in their places. It was the beach shaking, without being felt.

From the corner of his eye Colin saw a herd of creatures approach the water. He turned to look squarely at them, but they stayed where they could not be seen. It was impossible for him to understand quite what they were, how large or how many. The landscape was so odd here that the herd would not come where Colin could see it.

"Do you see them, Janet?" he said.

"They are inside my head," said Janet. "I suppose they are elephants." Neither of them had seen an elephant, but they felt it a likely name.

The herd came to the water, all tusks, horns, hide, hair, and waded in, lowered their heads, and drank. When they did so the water began to sink lower, and the light went from it, and the sun on the edge began to be further away. Now it seemed to both of them that here was the latest and last time of the whole world, and that nothing would or could be after this. It was a sorry time to be alone.

They hurried down towards the only living things they now knew, the strange herd of creatures that might be elephants, that would not walk fully into sight, but whether it was shyness or not, who knew?

The herd turned, and now that the animals in it looked straight at Colin and Janet, they could be seen. When they had not wanted to be seen they had not looked back and they had not been seen. It was as simple as that to understand.

But it was no easier to see the individual creatures. Great heads and bodies there were, and eyes and legs, teeth and tails, and all were coming up the beach from the sunken sea, with red sunlight strong on one side of them.

They came more and more stiffly, and then stood. They began to vanish, but only the heavy substance of them went, and there stayed the light frames of bone, standing beside the water, with the salt of the water crystal and glittering on the white backbones, the cages of rib, the pillars of legs.

The glitter became a dazzle, the dazzle a glare, the glare settled and resolved.

Straight ahead of Colin was Cathal, running over the tussocks of a moorland, stopping in his stride to run to him. Colin bent to touch his head, but straightened again when he heard his name called by his father, coming up a slope towards him.

I am out, Colin thought. I am away from that place. He

113

looked round for Janet, but she was not through with him. She should have come through, he thought. It is bad luck to her, and what is she to me?

He waved to his father, and took a step towards him, while Cathal stayed a little way off sniffing at him, sure and unsure.

Colin thought of Janet, locked away in a friendless land, alone, unhappy, abandoned. He could leave her, and it would never be known except to himself. It was not for that reason he turned about, and stepped back to Janet's side, and behind him Cathal and his father faded to nothing on the white beach. There was nowhere now for Colin to get out by.

"You have been this long time away," said Janet. It was so, he could see: the skeletons of the herd had fallen down on the shore, and started to become part of the land.

There, thought Colin, I have come back for her, because at last I have a liking for her, and she scolds me. I suppose I will bear with that. I hope it is for liking I came back; there is no other sense.

They went on, as they had been going, towards the herd, or the hills they had become, the rock they had changed to.

They were almost there, and wondering whether anything could be here for them, when Cathal touched the edge of Colin's hand with his nose.

"He has followed me through," said Colin.

"What has?" said Janet, and then she screamed.

Colin was doing what he would do if Cathal came to his hand like that: running his hand back to the dog's ear and scratching it. But something was wrong. He looked when Janet screamed. It was not Cathal, but an ugly, thin, sour dwarf, walking at his heels.

114

12

I am seeing badly, Colin thought. It is Cathal, not a dwarf.
The dwarf was there, and not there, not quite solid. Cathal
had been more solid a few minutes since. But Colin was
sure that it was Cathal, only seeming wrong.

The dwarf looked at Colin, looked away, and looked
again. He did what Colin had done, on seeing something
not very distinct. He sniffed. He did not like the smell of
Colin. Colin wondered whether he had seen, or listened
only.

They stood apart from one another. The dwarf bent,
picked up a cloudy stone and threw it at Colin. It hit him
like mist, and smoked to the ground. Colin laughed.

Janet shrieked again. "Leave it," she said. "Come away.
That is a bad thing, it will hurt you."

"It is throwing dust," said Colin. It might be throwing
dust, but it was growing angrier. And now it had been
joined by others like it, who began to throw insubstantial
pebbles too, that puffed on Colin and scattered to nothing.

Soon there was no doubt in Colin's mind that the dwarfs
were real: they became hard to his eye. In a little while
after that the stones they sent became hard to his skin, and
then heavy against his bone. He took a step backwards. He
had not expected things to be so firm and actual.

"Come away," said Janet. "Run. They will kill you."

115

It looked and felt as if they could. A stone knocked his cheek. He was cut inside by his own tooth, and tasted blood.

He turned, took Janet's hand, and ran. They ran among the fallen bones of the herd of animals, and found a hiding place in a ravine between two skulls. But they were discovered there, and made to move. They scrambled up a slope, where the drifted sand crept up a monstrous shoulder-blade, and sheltered under an overhang. Here, all the time, the white sand from the beach sprinkled down on them, and when the dwarfs came that way stones were flung.

Now they went back and back under the great bone, into a dark place, a cave, which they looked out from as well as they could, while a wind tore into the cave and made their eyes smart.

"I am bruised," said Colin.

"They were seeing me too," said Janet, with chattering teeth. "I wish I could safely lay hands on the little men. I would teach them throwing, of course."

"Hush now," said Colin. He listened. The wind was too strong to let them look, a constant cold stream. They walked backwards, listening forwards. There was a rattle at the mouth of the cave. The dwarfs were in.

"They cannot see us," said Janet.

It was true. But the dwarfs could hear. When she spoke a stone came tumbling near her, so that she stumbled back, falling into a litter of sticks and grass and dusty turf, that they both knew the taste of very well. At the cave mouth there was now a regular dry thumping, as the dwarfs built up the entry with stone and bone. No one would go out that way. After that the dwarfs made no sound.

The darkness stayed dark. Colin and Janet lost each other, by not staying in touch. Colin held a moving arm, and it was a dwarf's. Janet too had grasped one of them, but happily it was the same one. They managed to throw him down, and he went away.

After a long time, while they sat in the dark, close together, and getting colder, Colin thought they might be alone. Slowly, silently, he undid his wallet and brought

116

out the flint and steel, but not for now the tinder. Then, sharply, and while he looked at the distance ahead, he rattled out at knee-level a band of sparks.

The sparks showed the dwarfs listening. The light itself they did not see. Colin hammered out more sparks, and the dwarfs were blind to them, but listened for the knapping of blade on stone.

"They do not see," said Colin. At his words stones flew, but he and Janet bowed low and were not hurt. "We shall be able to."

He teased out some tinder, reached for the dry stuff they were sitting in, and had it ready. He struck sparks until one sat in the tinder, grew, and glowed. He breathed it larger still, drew it off into dry straw, raised it into a flame, transplanted it on to sticks, and had a fire. While the flame first stretched itself he and Janet stood aside in a fold of the cave wall. But it was not necessary; the dwarfs were blind to this fire too.

Colin fed it. The dwarfs heard the sticks move and snap. Colin lobbed a small stone over beyond them, and they turned to throw theirs that way too.

Colin studied the smoke. It was not rising, but going along the cave, deeper into it. "There is a way out," he said. "Make the fire large, and we shall walk in the smoke. Where it goes we shall go."

A dwarf came wandering and listening close to them. He did not see them; he did not see the fire. He walked through it, crunching but not spreading it. Colin would not consider brave what Janet did. She flung a stone at the dwarf's back. He did not feel it, but heard it when it fell to the floor. If it is not a fair fight then there is no bravery, Colin thought.

They took sticks and kindling with them: there might be a further fire to light on the way. Their lit fire lasted them for a long walk. As they went, feeling the floor of the cave in the dark, they turned to face the way they had come so that the smoke blew into their eyes and held them on course. The smoke at last died to nothing; there was no smell of it any longer. They fumbled along for a distance without it, but the draught alone on their eyes

117

was not enough. Colin picked up a loose stone and threw it off into the darkness. It landed, and echoed, but that was the only sound. There were no dwarfs present.

There they lit another fire with the rest of the wood. While they watched it take hold Colin drew out the chanter and played the three parts of the tune. Out of the echoes and stumbles of the cave had come to him a fourth part, the last airt. He was able to play it complete in his mind and fingers. The words were 'Breathing quiet days making songs.'

They went on again. "It is changed," said Janet. "Something happened when you played. I feel that I am alive." But Colin wondered what he felt, because you might be most alive when you are nearest death and cannot come out of the earth.

The dwarfs caught up with them. Stones fell beside them, and struck them.

"I will not be having the likes of that no more," said Janet. "There is this only to throw."

'Hush," said Colin.

"It is that bannock," said Janet. "It has been in your wallet. I shall give it again, yes, let them have it, I will," and she threw it. It went down towards the dwarfs and struck the ground. There was a flash of light, a shout of dwarf voices, and the cave closed up, taking away the breeze, the smoke, the way they had come.

Colin and Janet stood facing a cliff, in daylight, with the sea behind them, and in the sea a skin boat with a stone anchoring it.

"We shall never be home," said Janet. "Never."

"We are rid of the dwarfs," said Colin. "But this no doubt will be worse."

118

13

There was the skin boat, bobbing in slapping waves, and the same water washing their feet. Behind them was unbroken cliff, because the place they had come from was not there to be re-entered. To one side of the little cove they were in was a high slippery rock with weed. To the other a step or two of some steep little trod went up the rocks between the green fronds of bracken, green itself.

"It is the sea, no doubt," said Colin; "but we are not away yet, because that path is wrong and I will not take it. We must row the boat."

"I dare not do anything," said Janet. "I am without hope."

Colin looked at her. He would have to bring her away, and how could it be done? But she looked round her again, then at Colin, and smiled a smile that meant there was life even beyond hope.

"We will be getting the anchor up," she said. "Then when we are on the water I shall be wishing I was dead."

"That is for you to know," said Colin. They waded into the cold sea and lifted at the rope and at the stone, bringing it from the water and into its place in the boat. Then they got in it themselves, the movement clutching at their heads making them dizzy.

Colin put out the oars at once, because the boat was

turning broadside to the land. If it drove on, the skins could be cut and the boat sink. What they were in was real water without any mistake or fancy: the air was clear to its surface, and its wetness and cold could not be the make of a fairy charm; its salt tang made it real.

He rowed. He turned the boat stern to land, and struggled. Janet had out the other pair of oars, but she had only ever seen it done and not taken oars herself, so she made no useful going of it. Then she let go and slumped, and lay in the boat's bottom, seasick.

The boat moved dumpily in the water. There was a steepening and quickening of the waves, though not so hard or high that Colin could not row pretty well. Faransay began to recede. The little landing place they had been at became one of the many features of the shore. The ends of the island could be seen, with more sea to either side.

"We are away," said Colin. "Janet, we are away from it."

"Oh," said Janet, "oh, oh," and she lay where she was.

Colin rowed on. He turned his head and looked where he was going. There was land that must be home. He did not care where on the coast he came; from any place he could walk home, and so, no doubt, could Janet. But he thought she might stay at his house. He would remember not to take her in a boat, though she might travel better when she grew up.

As he turned his head back he thought he heard a call, a cry, not a word, but not an animal or bird either. It came again, from out of the island, and a third time. But we have got away, thought Colin. Surely, I hope. I must bring her home now.

He went on rowing. Faransay dropped further behind, further from Colin's eyes. Little by little the seas grew broader and flatter, the gentle swell breaking only occasionally into foam. Something broke the surface however, between boat and island. Something floated up and sank, and came again. Something approached.

It was a head, coming along at the top of the water, coming nearer, a white head. It was not fish or bird or seal; it was not any floating thing known to Colin.

His heart grew small inside him. His hands rested idly

120

on the oars. He waited for the escape to become nothing, for the grip of the island and the fairy people to close on them again.

"Are we there?" said Janet, feeling the boat sit differently on the water.

"No," said Colin. "We shall not get away now, we shall not escape. One of them is coming after us."

"Where is that?" said Janet. She sat up. "Oh," she said, "I am so ill in the boat; but I will be so and come home; I will not go back."

"There, see," said Colin. "That is a head coming at us, and what can we do for that? There will be a body with it, and I do not know what they will do, but they will take us back."

Janet looked for the white head, and found it clear against the water.

"We must row," she said. "I shall help now. I will leave these oars and sit beside you, and have one each. That thing is another deceit. You would not see it, but I do. They are sending the likeness of you after you; that thing is like you; but I tell you, we must not look at it, but only at the water near us, and must row."

Colin took one more look, however, and saw the head, and the water covering and uncovering it.

"They are walking on the bottom of the sea," he said.

"It would be easier swimming," said Janet.

"One is as easy as the other, for them," said Colin.

They rowed without looking back. Colin sat on the left side of the boat. He thought that he would pull more strongly than Janet, and would bring them nearer to the village, which lay over to the right, and further from the black cliff of the headland.

With two of them rowing the boat went along better. The following head was not gaining on them now. On the right the cliffs of the headland grew higher and closer, and the sea could be seen and heard boiling against them.

The sea flattened, all at once. One stroke had to fight to hold water, the next dropped into a sea smooth as batter.

"It is the current will take us home," said Colin. "But row, row, because it will bring the head too."

121

The head had a different idea. It came into the smooth water too, but went across it, and was lost among the black rocks at the shore below the cliffs, where spray rose every day of the year.

Colin and Janet changed places. Now he wanted to row to the left, on to the strand when they came to it. In a little while they did that, coming along the front of the village, and into shallow water. Colin put his oar down, jumped over the side, and pulled the boat on to the shingle. Janet followed him out, and they both stood there shivering, the boat trembling too at the water still running under. They brought the anchor from its place and dropped it over the side.

"We are home," said Janet. "There is my house; but my mother will be at the island. Well, there will be people about. She will scold me, coming back here with you."

"I do not know you," said Colin. "How could you live here? It is where I live. You do not come from here."

"You must come from another place," said Janet. "This is my home."

An old dog came waddling down the strand, sniffing at them. It took no notice of Janet, but breathed deeply at Colin, heaved itself up and put its front feet on his arm, and sang at him with love.

"It is like Cathal," said Colin. "But it is not." However, the dog walked at his heel like Cathal, touching his hand with its nose. "I do not know," said Colin. "I do not."

Up among the houses a bell began to ring.

"We are days late," said Janet. "It is the Sabbath kirk bell."

14

"I will not be going in the kirk," said Colin. "It is all to be looked at. I do not understand who you are; I daresay there are kirks in the fairy land, and I will be trusting nothing."

"But I will be trusting you," said Janet.

They walked up the strand. Janet was sure she was home. Colin was sure he was not: the only thing that might have made him sure was Cathal, and this dog could not be Cathal, who was at the island in any case. We are enchanted yet, he thought; we are not out of it.

A very old man came out of a house, bending low in the doorway, and putting a slow arm to the turf roof to hold himself up. Under his other arm the old man carried bagpipes, the limb-like drones and chanter dangling.

"Alasdair's house," said Janet. "Who that will be I do not know. Oh Colin, I feel that strangeness, oh, what is it?"

The very old man waited for them. Further up the village the bell stopped ringing.

Then, padding over the strand, came a man, his clothes wet against him, his head white under the sky. He came up to Colin and gave him a thump between the shoulder blades, and then shouted at him a word that was not a word.

"Duncan," said Colin. Duncan it was, with his head

washed white as he swam from the island after the boat, landing along the coast and running here. Now, unable to make clear sounds, he was mouthing a shape that did not mean 'Colin', angrily going through his sets of sign language.

"What is it?" said Janet. "Who?"

"It is my uncle," said Colin. "I think it was his boat we took. He is telling me something. I do not know what. He is deaf and dumb, and he is saying my wrong name."

The very old man had come down to them now. He laid a hand on Duncan, to calm him, and to keep himself up.

"Well, Colin, it is a long time," said the old man. "We have been waiting. Duncan here thinks you are Donal. No, do not shake your head," because Colin had done that, to settle what he had heard into what he could understand. "You have been away seven years, and a little more, so Donal is up at your size. I have waited for you. But I have waited longer for others, and all of my life for one."

Singing began in the church.

"Colin," said the old man to Duncan, "Colin. I said, all will not return; all shall come back."

Duncan understood. He gave Colin a great holding hug, and ran off, towards the kirk. At the same time Colin understood that the very old man was Alasdair, and that Janet was the girl he had lost on the island many more years ago than seven.

"Alasdair," he said. "It is not canny."

"Indeed not," said Alasdair. "I have waited to give you the pipes."

"Yes," said Colin. "This is Janet."

"Aye," said Alasdair. "Well, so it is; but that is the way of things, Colin. I am out of my time as much as she is, and there is nothing to be done. Now be blowing up that bag, and take your last lesson of me, Sabbath day or not. It will not be a kirk day, when Duncan has said his catechism yonder."

"Alasdair," said Janet. "The piper lad."

"Forty-nine years," said Alasdair. "What did you do, lassie, that took so long?"

"You could not know," said Colin, between breaths

into the pipes. The bag was filling, and he pressed with his elbow at the thing tucked under his arm. The drones began to skirl.

Then, as he was about to play, he paused, and his hand went to his wallet, and pulled from it the dark and ivory chanter he found at the island those few days, those seven years, since. He put it in the socket in the bag, and the elderwood reed shook and shrilled and sounded. Now, playing, there came from his fingers the four airts of the tune of the island. He had not known how much they were with him, how well they had stayed in his fingers.

Duncan brought the people out of the kirk as Colin began. They stood round Colin, waiting to speak until he finished.

But it was not Colin they watched, because a graver and stranger thing was happening while he played.

Janet and Alasdair had moved aside a little, so that Alasdair could sit against the house.

There, before them all, as the tune was playing, Janet was growing up from being a child to a young woman, and then an older one, then elderly, and at last aged. And in the wind coming down the strand, as she stood there, having grown tall, and looking at them sweetly and troubled, and then stooping with age and looking at them with sorrow, and holding out a hand towards Alasdair, in that long sea wind she began to blow away, dissolving to a fine pure dust vanishing along the shore and up towards the hills.

Colin watched as he played. He could not stop what he was doing, but with his heart he longed to keep her, longed for her to stay, because it had been for her that he had made hard choices, and with her he had struggled seven years, though they felt like no time, no part of time at all.

As she went, her smile turning from sorrow to joy as she did, he perceived that she was still part of that other land she had been in so long. He saw that the reality of her was not here in the village, that the shape he saw was of someone in another place; that he was seeing through her the land of the fairy people still.

The tune ended. Janet was no more amongst them. Alasdair had closed his eyes too, and what could go with her had gone. The men made to bring him into his house, but Colin set down the pipes, and while they groaned on the ground he went to carry Alasdair himself. He had felt, and known, as he played, as Janet went through the span of her life, that he was growing through his. He had not time to think, until afterwards, that he might be about to go into dust himself. When he had not done so he felt regret at not going with Janet. But then he had seen Alasdair pass from the world with her, and knew he should not do so himself, for with three there is less than half each.

In Alasdair's house he laid among Alasdair's clothes the dark chanter from the island. Now, played for the last time, it lay cracked and crooked, ebony split, ivory crazed, no longer bright, no longer true and voiced, not much more than a twig. He had been childish, he thought, to take it up. And when he had put it down he could not see in that place any more, because there was a crack of shadow over his sight.

He came out, and could see either side of that crack, but in it saw distant other lands. A boy was given him to hold. It was Donal. Donal called to be set down, and became shy, hiding behind his mother's shawl, and she was shy too.

"Well now," she said, "I have knitted up wool for a waistcoat each year, and pulled it out, so come your ways home and fit it. We have known you would come, because we have seen you many times. And you will have to be taking peats from your bedstead, as I told you before you went."

"Ah mother," said Colin, and his voice was strange to him, "you told me so this morning only. I have not had my dinner yet," and he showed them his wallet, with the oatcake, the cheese, and the leaf of cabbage.

Cathal ate them, leaving the cabbage leaf; for the old dog was indeed Cathal.

15

Colin had grief as well as wonder at so much time passed so soon and lost.

"It is nothing for you," said his mother. "You are back again in your time. But for Janet, why there was only Alasdair, and no other people. She was gone before your father was born. But are you seven years tired, holding your head and your eyes like that?"

"I am dizzy with coming home," said Colin; and he thought it might be so, but it was his seeing that troubled him, with a patch down the world now as if the middle of a page were torn out and the next showed through, reading no sense.

"It is no wonder, Colin Henderson," said his mother. "Sit against the hearth." She brought him what she had knitted year by year when he was not there, and put it on him. It fitted close as home. She cut for him from the week's baking of the day before. To him it was his dinner come late, so late he did not know how to swallow, and sat there grinding a crust like a cow with her cud, until the bread would be taken down of its own accord. Then he told his mother how time had passed in the long day he had been gone.

After that he slept on the chair. When he woke his mother said, "You had need of that. You have been seven years waking, however you count it. Now there are two things: Mrs MacDonald will be seeing you at her house; and there is a girl up on the hill has been sore for the sight of you longer than you have been gone."

"I will take the chance of that," said Colin, "now I am sure this is home."

"We have all been sore for the sight of you," said Mrs Henderson. "What else will this be but home?"

In that day he walked to Mrs MacDonald's slate-roofed house to be looked at by her. She said it was a strange tale enough, and that he should forget it or think of a better. But she was glad, she said, that there was to be a piper again in the village, and he was to go to Strath and learn all the tunes, some new, some old. Colin thought it best to say nothing of any he had come home with.

He was met by a girl he did not now know. Like Donal, she had grown up since he last saw her: the adults had changed a little, the children much.

"We used to drive the cows together," she said.

"You are Anabel Tivert," he said.

"You will have been thinking of me all these years," she said. "I have thought upon you every day and every night both before and after you went, and I shall do so again."

"For all that," said Colin, "if I had known I would have forgotten you if I could, as I remember you now; indeed you were nothing to me."

"What of that?" said Anabel. "I knew it."

"That was then," said Colin. "And it would have been a pity, for now I see that you were there for me. But I have been looking at another girl with more than care, and that lasted longer than I knew, and now it is over with, except the remembering."

"When you brought her back," said Anabel, "I saw that neither of us had anything to say to the other, and that was the way of it. But now she has gone I think that anything you gave her has been given back to you and you may let me have it if you wish; and I should wish it too. I felt peace for her."

"As to that," said Colin, "I think we have been well apart, and could be well together. Now that Alasdair's house is empty, and when he is taken from it, we can live there: my mother may keep my bedstead full of turf; and my father has no need of me: he has Donal."

Colin had to empty his bedstead, however. Duncan, having been so long in the water swimming from the island, became fevered and ill, and lay in it all summer. He got up when the autumn came, and now his hair grew out from his bald head white like cotton, and he sat smiling by the fires of the village, now and then going into a dream of his own and telling what was to happen.

Colin became the piper. He did as Mrs MacDonald said, going to other places for tunes and for learning the music, the reels and laments, the great music, the middle music, and the small, and their own 'The Keppoch Rade'. That was his life. But the four airts of the tune he brought from Faransay were the best he was given and the best he gave.

He and Anabel came to live in Alasdair's house. Always across Colin's eyes was the streak of another world. As the years went by that streak became wider, and he was still young when he could no longer see this world. The rest of this world called him blind, but he knew what he saw, whether it was the dancing floor of the fairies, the sweet glades of grass, the dead salt of the last sea, the dark of the cave with the fire smoke, or the welcome love of the fairy King and Queen.

At last he needed this world no more. At one September new moon he took his pipes to the island, and stayed there, year after year alone, or for a time now and then with one of his sons, young Alasdair, coming in and out of the fairy lands, telling of one place in the other, until he stayed there always. Cathal, who ate the oatcake that lay with the bannock, had gone to the fairies years before, and waited for Colin, to journey with him now, whatever side of life he was.

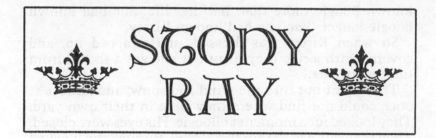

STONY RAY

1

There were eight cats in the show. Seven of them came in, but black Boogie stayed where he was, lying under the wall beside the grindstone, in a sheltered place.

Kirsty knew what had happened. He had died. She knew at once. Mum knew as well.

They looked at each other.

"Put some clothes on," said Mum.

"Yes," said Kirsty. She came back from the doorway and Mum closed the door. Kirsty stood by the stove and got dressed. Some snow on her foot changed into a blister of water. "I didn't have to worry," she said. "I didn't have to think if he was all right. He wasn't poorly."

"Just very old," said Mum.

"Older than Grandpa," said Kirsty.

"A lot older," said Mum. "If Grandpa was a cat too."

"I'm cold," said Kirsty. "I'm feeling his coldness."

"I know," said Mum. "But he isn't there to feel it."

"I've got the cold of where he isn't sitting by me any more, as well," said Kirsty.

"That's the one I have," said Mum. "After breakfast we'll ask Dad or Grandpa to see to him."

But Kirsty thought she would like to see to him herself. Mum thought she wanted to do it too, because she had known Boogie more than half her life. She had known Boogie longer than she had known Kirsty.

So when Kirsty was dressed, and wrapped up, and covered with a rug, they went out and got a shovel from the tractor box.

They went out into the wind and snow, and almost at once could not find where they were in their own yard. They looked for a moment at Boogie. His eyes were closed. Then they dug a path into the garden, through the blocked up stile.

Then they had problems. The garden was so wild with driven snow that they could hardly move about. Here they could not tell where they were at all. They were in a white bowl stirred by a storm, and the flying snow was not in flakes and powder but in stinging lumps.

Then Mum turned her back to the weather and dug through the snow to find the ground. She had to dig again to make a place to put the dug earth. All the time the snow fell in the hole again, so she was always digging through whiteness.

They went back for Boogie.

"What are you at?" said Dad, going through the yard then with a pail of steaming milk, and opening the kitchen door.

"Tip some out for the rest," said Mum. "They've had nothing."

"I will," said Dad. He stood in the doorway for a moment and dipped a cup in the pail and put milk in the cats' bowl. They all ran to it. But then Thingy turned away from the milk and came across the yard. Chang came part of the way and then turned back for a mouthful of milk first. Thingy came on and spoke to Boogie.

"Come away out of it," said Dad, because he wanted to close the door and Chang was in it, coming halfway out and going back for another lap at the bowl.

"They know," said Mum. "They feel it too. They think different things about it, don't you?" and she put a snowy hand down to Thingy's head. Thingy pushed against the hand, and gave Boogie a lick.

Mum took Boogie up and into the fierce garden. Kirsty

held his limp weight while Mum scraped snow from the hole. Then she put him in, and each gave him a last smoothe, while Thingy stood attentively by.

"That's tidy," said Mum. Thingy came down from a heap of snow and looked. "I think it's snow in my eyes," said Mum. Kirsty thought her own eyes had tears in them, warmer than snow.

They walked back out of the garden that was a wilderness of snow, into a yard that seemed calm and peaceful, and then into the kitchen, which seemed as warm and still as something that had never known movement. "And I sometimes feel it is draughty in here," said Mum.

Chang had been waiting for them in the yard. People from Siam are not expected to go into the coldest places in the world, Mum said. She shook snow from Kirsty's rug, and Kirsty was dry under it.

"Now, look at that," said Mum. "Some of them don't care at all." Clara had climbed up on the rack above the stove, and was taking over Boogie's own place and settling to sleep. "She knows and she doesn't care."

Thingy jumped up on the edge of the stove and stood on his hind legs to look at the place where Boogie had always been. Clara turned her face to him, thought for a moment, opened her mouth and hissed, looked at Mum and Kirsty, and put her head down again. Thingy came down and licked at the dry milk bowl.

"We can all have breakfast," said Mum, and began getting it ready. "We'll have ours, and the men when they come in, because you know how long it takes outside this weather."

Before the men came in, before breakfast was over, Granny rang up. Granny was Dad's mother, and she had retired away from the farm. Grandpa was Mum's father, and he lived here. Kirsty was related to them twice as much as usual because Dad and Mum were cousins. Dad had always lived in this house, and Mum next door. Grandpa had moved from next door as well, and there was a whole empty house left in case it was ever useful.

Granny wanted to know what the weather was like up there. Her newspaper was late, and the school was closed.

Mum told her about Boogie. Granny said that her very old greyhound, Patch, hated the snow, and stood there trembling instead of walking about and keeping warm. She thought she should make him a thicker jacket. More than that, she thought Kirsty should come down and stay because she thought the weather would get worse and the farm would be blocked in and Kirsty ought to go to school.

That was Kirsty's part of the call. Then she and Mum talked a bit about Grandpa, and how he was. Mum said he seemed a bit down, but he was well, and the weather didn't bother him. Granny said there might be something fretting him, from what she had heard, and Mum changed the conversation to the weather again, and ended it by running a tape-measure round Kirsty to help when Granny was making something. A dog jacket, Mum said.

Breakfast was over. They were warm again. The men were still outside. Kirsty put on her boots and coat again and went out to see to her calf, Princess Marina. Princess Marina was like Chang, creamy all over, with dark ears and tip to her tail. But she had always been too big to sleep on Kirsty's bed with her.

Kirsty crossed the yard again. The track they had dug to the garden was full, and so was the stile. But she was not going that way with her feet, only with a thought.

Her feet took her to the calf house, dark and warm and full of breath. Grandpa was in there.

"There's nothing to do here," he said. He was not at all pleased. "I've done it all for you. It's got to be done. You can't stop inside out of the weather when there's stock to tend. You should have been here long since." Then he went out into the yard and left Kirsty in the dark. She heard the wind laugh and the pail handle clank, and then there was only the sound of the calves chewing hay.

"He wants his breakfast too," she said to Princess Marina. The Princess put out her tongue and took up a wisp of hay and moved her back feet. Kirsty rubbed her between the ears and then left her. Everything had been done for her, and Kirsty had used up all her animal feeling for the time being, after burying Boogie and understanding

134

what Thingy felt and knowing what Clara had done. There was nothing more to think.

She was wrong about Grandpa wanting his breakfast. When she went in he was sitting by the stove and drinking a cup of tea. But he only drank half of it, then put it down and said he wanted no more. Thingy came to look at it.

Grandpa got up and said he was off to bed. Mum asked whether he was poorly. Grandpa was quite sharp with her, too.

"You'd not know," he said.

"You could say," said Mum. "You could speak. You've been the wrong end out for long enough."

"I'll think on," said Grandpa. "But I'll go to bed now. I need nothing, so I don't need seeing to."

"I'll just see you're comfortable," said Mum.

"No need," said Grandpa. "I can get myself in bed."

"I'll see you in," said Kirsty. She thought she could help people, even if not animals just at the moment.

"Nobody," said Grandpa. "I don't need anyone. Leave me alone." And he went out of the room.

"One of his turns," said Mum. "Something and nothing, and we're the worse off for it. Your father can eat two breakfasts."

"Is it my fault?" said Kirsty.

"I don't know," said Mum, cross with something else and carefully, or carelessly, burning the bacon. "Oh, look at the stuff. Here you are, Thingy. Oh, I'm no good at this job."

"You are," said Kirsty, going to lean against her at the stove. Mum put a fresh piece of bacon in the pan, and then brought Clara down and hugged her.

I think she likes the cats best, thought Kirsty. They don't cause things. "Did I do it?" she asked again.

"I don't know," said Mum in her desperate way that she sometimes had. "Did you say something nasty?"

"Nothing," said Kirsty. Clara licked Mum's fingers and looked down at the bacon and then at Thingy who was eating some, and Chang who was wishing he was.

"I was late feeding Princess Marina, and he'd done it," said Kirsty. "That's all."

"He likes everything down on the dot," said Mum. "More than most." She put Clara back on the shelf over the stove and told her to live on the smell of bacon. "But it's not just that, and if it was it isn't your fault. I think his girl-friend's playing him up."

Grandpa had a girl-friend or two. Kirsty could remember one that had come to the farm a long time ago, and no one had liked her, not even Grandpa. They could all smell her scent for days after. So it wasn't that one any more.

"He'll get painted into a corner one day," Mum said, turning the bacon and making the other side buzz. "He's young yet, you know, and if he wasn't, you're never too old. But he isn't strong, just like a little straw in his body and thin like water in his life. It's worst in the snow, after he nearly died in it once."

Kirsty thought of him black and small in the yard, like Boogie. She knew how he had been found in a drift under a wall when he was a lad, and been brought next door and warmed better.

Boogie had gone further than that. Grandpa was still here a long time later. "He wouldn't be in the snow at all if he went off with one of them," said Kirsty.

"But what would he go to?" said Mum. "I think he's got a right one now, that Betty, with no more feeling than a gate-stoup, just altogether too plain in her senses."

Then the door opened and Dad came in, snow on him and snow following and a puff of wind that made the cats look round.

"Is Uncle Fred outside yet?" said Dad. "I thought he'd done."

"Gone to bed," said Mum. "He's bad. Poorly."

"One of his turns?" said Dad. "Now's a fine time. Whether I'll get the milk away I don't know, in all this. Is that my breakfast, Mother?"

"Eat both," said Mum. "He wanted nothing. I'll go up and see what he's doing. I'll take the hot water for a bottle for him and you can boil it again for your tea."

"Aye," said Dad. "Do that. I'm not out of these clothes yet."

So Mum filled a hot water bottle and went upstairs with it and Dad got his working clothes off. First his cap went up against Clara and began to drip on her and on the stove. His sheepskin mittens went on the back of the stove and stood there steaming. A trickle of water went down to the hot-plate and hissed. His woollen gloves went up on Chang, at the other end of the rack from Clara. His waterproof outer coat, with the waterproof worn out and snow inside

137

as well, went on a chair beside the long electric radiator, and Hubert and Kitten had to move from their places when snow fell on them. Snowy and Candy got up offended when a wet jacket was put the other side of the same radiator. They sat by the stove for a moment, but then they were replaced by wet boots.

"Booted out," said Kirsty.

"Well, happen they are," said Dad. Then his waterproof trousers were hung on the rail and there was no more stove left to be in front of. Then one sock went on Clara and another on Chang.

"Shifted the lot," said Dad, cheerfully. It wasn't often he could tease all the cats without trying. The last one was Thingy, who was on his chair.

The cats stood round the floor, waiting for something good to happen. Chang reached up and rattled the knife handles on the table. He knew that had something to do with food.

Kirsty made the tea. Dad washed his hands. Upstairs Mum could be heard talking to Grandpa, but he could not be heard talking to her. Perhaps he was saying nothing.

Perhaps, thought Kirsty, he has nothing to say. Perhaps he can't talk any more.

Then no one was saying anything. There's nothing happening inside me, and nothing outside, thought Kirsty. Dad is eating his bacon. Cats are standing round the room. Mum is upstairs. Grandpa probably is but I am not thinking about that. Boogie is outside. I am not here. I have stopped being here. Or nothing is real.

"You've a long face on you," said Dad. "This bacon got a bit cracked in the pan. Come here, Fang, and get a bit."

"Chang," said Kirsty. "Not Fang." But she felt better, because if there is something wrong, like Chang being called Fang, then there is something for it to be wrong against, and what it was wrong against was what she knew was right; so she must be there to think it. "I'm here," she said.

"You're like him," said Dad. "Coming and going a bit."

Mum came down while he was saying that. "Going a bit now, I think," she said, and stood there by the stove and blew her nose four times and wiped her eyes. "He doesn't think he's got long for here. I've never seen him like it. But I have, I suppose."

"I'll go and look at him," said Dad. "Right now."

So he got up from the table, pulled on his slippers, and went upstairs in his shirtsleeves.

"Now then," said Mum. "That's what he'll say."

"Now then," said Dad upstairs. "What ails you, Uncle Fred?"

Dad upstairs said, "Well, can't you wait? This isn't the best time of year for that sort of thing."

Kirsty started to tidy up the breakfast table, "I'm near on to laugh," she said. "What's he talking about?"

"That's your Dad," said Mum. "If it doesn't suit farming you haven't to do it. He's a right simple man, your Dad. And mine is right stubborn."

"You haven't to do it," said Dad upstairs. "Be reasonable. Just give a thought."

"Simple," said Mum, "and set in his ways. Just after haytime and he wouldn't have minded. Might just save him the trouble of going on holiday." Then she started washing up, and Dad could no longer be heard, except for the last thing he said, "Think on, Uncle Fred, think on."

When he came down he said, "It's starvation cold up there. We should get him a fire in the room. Well then, I had a word with him. You've just got to get him to change his mind and he'll be right. He just wants to be off, that's all."

"We'd best get him a doctor," said Mum.

"He isn't a doctor case," said Dad. "But you'd best telephone and see if he wants to come."

"He won't want," said Mum. "But he'll have to."

Dad began putting on his wet clothes again. "I've to take the milk," he said. "If I can get down the road. If I see the doctor I'll fetch him along, tell him. Kirsty, you go up and talk with him up there. He's all for saying goodbye, but don't take notice of that."

"We'll both go up," said Mum. "Bring a few sticks, and wait while I telephone down."

Dad went out. The tractor drummed its way out of the

139

yard and the yard dog barked and ran behind it biting the snow. Mum telephoned the surgery and explained she couldn't help about the weather, which the surgery quite understood. Then Mum put the telephone down and looked at it. "It's asleep most of the time," she said. "It's like a sleeping foot that's got in the house from outside there. A talking foot in the door."

Then she got some sensible black coal, and they went upstairs. Grandpa lay on his back, looking at the ceiling.

"Not a word," said Mum. "We'll get you a fire lit, and the doctor to you."

"They'll neither of them do anything for me," said Grandpa. "But do it if you like. This is the weather I came here in, in the snow, I came wandering through the snow. I was brought here, you know. The snow brought me here. Stony Ray and the snow."

"You're daft, you," said Mum. "Lie there and say nowt." She pulled the screen from the fireplace and put paper in the grate and stood a lit match under it and heaped sticks on the paper. Grandpa closed his eyes. "That'll be grand for the doctor," he said.

"Go to sleep," said Mum, crossly. She and Kirsty stayed by the fire until they were warmed by it, and then they left the room.

Not long afterwards the tractor came back. It stopped in the yard. There was a clatter of things being laid against the house wall, and the doctor came in, in a woollen hat. "What is it?" he said. "James gave me a ride up, and I've skis to go down on. I can tell you, it's what I wanted, to come up to Stony Ray on a day like this. We'll have some tea first."

3

When the woollen hat came off his head steamed. So did his cup of tea. "Too many cats," he said, looking round the kitchen. Then the sun came out and shone on the steam and on his head and made the kitchen window look pretty but very dirty. "You wouldn't think it could come out on a day like this," he said. "Now, where's the patient?"

He and Mum went upstairs. Kirsty looked outside. The cats looked with her. Then all of them went out. The cats' eyes went down to upright slits and Kirsty's eyes ached, with the brightness of sun on snow.

The wind had gone almost away. Now and then the air rolled over on itself, and that was all. Kirsty went back in and put on her boots, coat, and gloves. The rug wasn't needed. She went out again and stamped her way to the stile into the garden, to see how Boogie was getting on.

The stile was blocked up. She stood on the stone step of it and looked over without going through. The garden was smooth and white, as if no one had ever been in it. Even the tall things were loaded down flat with snow. Now and then a lump of snow fell away and a stem lifted itself. Otherwise it was all peaceful and quite a comfortable place. But Kirsty thought there ought to be a few paw prints belonging to Boogie.

Then she went back and had a look at the doctor's red

skis, standing against the wall beside the kitchen door. In the room above she heard the doctor talking.

She went round the other side of the house, where the tractor had been, treading through the shaped place where its body and the bottom of the engine had touched the snow. Her eyes had become used to the brightness now, and she could see the blue shadows under the sunlight, and brighter blue sky beyond the snow. The snow was golden in the sunshine; the walls were grey, the farm gates were red. There was the Brough, the mountain belonging to the farm, capped with blown snow, and the far side of the dale beyond, and round and up the hillside the smooth snow with a hard edge across the Mire, and up to Stony Ray, usually a heap of grey stone with a tall pillar, but now a white monument. Then there was the fellside called the Stake with a whisper of a road going up it, as if a stick had been laid gently there for a moment. Then came the trees leafed with snow and the house. All over the snow, where the wind rolled, there was a stirring and movement, where the flakes blew, and a fuzziness. Kirsty wondered at first whether her eyes were going wrong, but it was the ground going wrong.

And down the other way the road went to the village, tractor-rutted. Kirsty thought of going down with the doctor. A ski each, she wondered; could it be done? Then she was too late. He came round the corner, strangely stretched in all directions, long feet before and after him, long rods to his arms, and looking even more extended because he had his hands to his head, adjusting the woollen hat. He sledged himself off down the road.

Pulling me on a toboggan, thought Kirsty. But he isn't.

But the road was there; and there was nothing to do up here. Kirsty felt she would not be so stuck to the place if she got to Granny's house. The road was the long way to Granny's house. The short, easy way was to go across between the Brough and the Mire, and down over the moor. Kirsty remembered going there once on her own for the afternoon, without telling anyone, and being back for tea, and nobody minded till Granny told them on the telephone.

142

Mum was in the kitchen, and the table was getting a scrub.

"It's the weather," said Mum. "Better in hospital, he said."

"What's wrong with it?" said Kirsty. "Wind?"

"No," said Mum. "Grandpa. Doctor wants him down at Northallerton for a bit, to keep an eye on him."

"He must be bad," said Kirsty. She didn't want to hear of anything changing, although there was nothing to do when everything was the same.

"No," said Mum, grinding off the surface of the table with the brush. "But just in case. If we get really blocked in and he does get worse, then we can't do anything. Doctor's gone to arrange for the ambulance."

Kirsty knew what to do. Everything had been arranged for her quite simply. She went up to her room, at the second attempt, because the first time she was called back to take off her snow-laden boots. When she was up there she packed her bag, trousers, socks, shirts, skirts, hairbrush, pink panther, whale with pyjamas in, black dangling spider, Opal fruits, bottle of scent, green necklace, green bangle, umbrella, all her metal money, winter knitting (really a scarf for the panther, but Mum said it resembled a row of buttonholes), a packet of tissues, and a picture of nearly all the cats (two were only tails waving, and one was pretending not to be there at all, though he was at the time – Chang).

Then she went to sit by Grandpa's fire. He was perched up now, and had been drinking a cup of tea.

"You off?" he said, after a time of looking at her.

"I'm going down with you in the ambulance," said Kirsty.

"That's it, is it?" said Grandpa.

"I'll go to Granny's for a bit," said Kirsty.

"Ambulance," said Grandpa.

Downstairs the telephone rang. Mum stopped scrubbing the table and went to it, and started saying "Yes"; and "I suppose".

"I'm not ill," said Grandpa. "I'm just dying. I've done it before, and this time I'm going to."

"You won't," said Kirsty, but she wondered. "And you have to do it down there."

Downstairs Mum was leaving the telephone and going out for Dad and making him come in at once. He came in and said "Yes?" to the telephone. "I can do that," he said. "I can near on do it. It won't be quiet it, not quiet. I'll do my best. I'll listen out, and I'll put small coal on the fire, slack, and make black smoke. Black smoke. They're fools on the telephone," he added, when he had put it down. "I'll be off and do that."

So he went out again and on the tractor. Mum went out, not finishing the scrubbing, and could be heard raking about in the coal hole.

Kirsty left her bag and went downstairs. She telephoned Granny, and said she was coming down in the ambulance when they took Grandpa off, and it might be in time for dinner, so keep it hot.

She went upstairs again. Grandpa's room was the waiting room for this journey. There was wet on the window, and through it she could see something moving about in a field. She wiped a pane clean. In the four-acre, between the house and Stony Ray, was the tractor, going round in a large circle, and when it had completed it it backed up a bit and went across the middle, round a quarter again, and across the middle again. The design showed up in shadow. Then the tractor came to the edge of the field and Dad walked back to the house.

"What's he doing?" said Grandpa.

"Foddering snow," said Kirsty. "Gone for a ride out in it. I don't know."

Dad came in. He took off his boots downstairs and came up, rubbing his hands.

"That's all fit up," he said. "They can't miss it. Wait on; I've to get the slack." He went down again, and came up with a bucket of coal dust and put it down cold by the fire.

"You'll be right, down there," he said to Grandpa. "All the pretty nurses, you'll be right. But they can't get the ambulance up the bank."

"That's that, then," said Grandpa.

"I could take you down in the tractor box," said Dad.

144

"On a couple of sacks and some hay, and a sup of whisky first."

Grandpa said nothing. If things were too ridiculous he kept quiet. "Just the whisky," he said. That part seemed sensible to him.

"So they're sending a helicopter," said Dad. "It's to land out in the four-acre where I've marked it."

Mum shouted from downstairs. "It's coming. I can hear it."

They could hear it upstairs too, whipping and cracking its way across the sky. Dad picked up the bucket of coal dust and flung some on the fire. Usually a little smoke gets into the room when that is done. Today the helicopter was just overhead and the wind of it pushed a whole chimney of smoke down again and set everything running the wrong way. The room became black with smoke and soot and gritty dust, and there was darkness for a time, and the house trembled and the helicopter roared.

Dad dragged the window open and cold air came in and black air went out. In the four-acre the helicopter disappeared in its own white cloud and then was sitting in the circle.

Grandpa was under the clothes. "I'm not going," he said. "Not in that."

"Just a flying tractor," said Dad. "Tractor."

"I haven't to be touched," said Grandpa, coughing under his pillows. "It's my life and I'll live it, and it's my death and I'll die it." And the greasy dust settled on the sheets.

4

Mucky, thought Kirsty. This is all mucky. A great thing of black grease, like a daddy-long-legs, came down through the air and landed on her sleeve. It smudged in when she brushed it away. Another came down on her hair, and she saw it tie itself round several strands and make a dirty knot.

Horrible, also, she thought. Poor Grandpa, hiding in his own bed because we are all throwing him out. Like Chang being put out in the rain when he didn't want to go. Not quite so bad, though, because Chang would be picked up and thrown out so that the door could be closed before he got to the ground. Kirsty looked from the window. The cloud of smoke had gone away. The white rising of snow had fallen round the helicopter. The trees by the house were moving still and snow had fallen from them and they were leafless of it.

Annoying was the other thing Kirsty had in mind. If Grandpa didn't go then there was no room for her to have a lift down to Granny's. Granny had a shampoo, and a spray that went on the taps. Mum used a jug.

Three men came out of the helicopter. They came out low, because the big blades were still whirling above it, and they were pulling a rolled-up stretcher.

"They're rescue people," said Kirsty. "You should go with them."

"I don't need to get rescued," said Grandpa. "I can lie here." Then he coughed and coughed.

"I'll be off and bring them in," said Dad.

"What a mess," said Mum. "What will they think? But I'll have to put it right when they've gone."

"They don't need to come in," said Grandpa.

"Sit up," said Mum. She went round the room putting it right. Down went the window, and the fire, all black dust, sent out another black breath. "No you don't," said Mum, getting at it with the poker and breaking through the black to the red fire below. Kirsty, still looking from the window at Dad meeting the three men from the helicopter, saw the smoke cross the sky overhead, the proper signal Dad had tried to make before.

"Now sit up," said Mum. Grandpa took no notice. Two cats came into the room and sat by the fire. Kirsty went and stood by them, beside her bag with the things in for staying with Granny.

Mum picked up Grandpa's quilt, gave it a shake, and put it on the bed again. The room had begun to look normal, or better than normal, since it had a burning fire.

"We have to get you ready," said Mum. "Have you got your teeth in?"

Mum pulled down the top sheet and turned it over. "Oh," she said, that'll take some washing. What a grime there is. But I'll do it when ..." But then she began to wonder what she wanted to say.

"When you've gone," said Kirsty, finishing the words for her. But when she had said them she knew why Mum had stopped before they came out.

There was Grandpa looking at them, and raising his head a little so that Mum could shake his pillows. Mum was thinking that she did not want him to go. Sending him away in a helicopter might be the modern thing to do, but it was still not natural. He didn't want to go, and it was not natural.

"You want to stop here, don't you?" she said.

"It doesn't look safe to me," said Kirsty. There was nothing to stop the helicopter giving her a lift down, even if Grandpa was not in it with her.

147

"Don't get soft," said Grandpa. "I'll stop because I want to, not because you ask me. I'll say what I do."

"Don't get typical," said Mum. "Or you *will* go. But I know there's nothing wrong with you. Don't we, Kirsty?"

"We don't think there is," said Kirsty. "The only thing slightly wrong with you is you won't go in the helicopter so I can have a ride down to Granny's." By now she had begun to think there would be no chance of asking for a ride without him. She felt that the helicopter men might not be listening.

They were coming now, in at the door, and across the kitchen and up the stairs. Two cats went under the bed.

Grandpa said nothing. Kirsty knew exactly what he meant by saying nothing. He meant that he agreed there was nothing wrong with him, but all the same the right thing to do was go to bed and cure it; and that he didn't want any sympathy, only some attention. If he went away he might stop being there at all. Anybody could understand that. Even a cat knew about it. Chang was very good at it. In fact he was an expert. Once when he had to be taken to the vet with a bad leg that Mum could hear broken bones in, the box he was in had arrived empty, and when they came back he was on the roof completely cured.

By now the room was full of people. It was the Army in flying helmets, undoing its stretcher and taking up all the space and beginning to surround Grandpa.

"Would you like a cup of tea?" said Mum.

There was a flurry and a thump under the bed, then a scream. Somebody had trodden on Kitten's tail, and Kitten went downstairs fast.

"No thank you, ma'am," said one of the men. "We'll just get our stretcher alongside the bed. He'll be quite warm. Is this bag to go?"

"No, that's mine," said Kirsty. Then she was just wondering whether she should ask about a lift, when Dad said:

"Come away, Mother, these lads want to be that side of the bed, they can't lift him out the wall side."

"He doesn't want to go," said Mum.

"He doesn't have the say-so," said Dad. "Let's be having you, Uncle Fred."

"I said before," said Grandpa. "I'm not off."

"We've come for you," said one of the men. "Hospital must be the right place for you, or they wouldn't send us."

"My daughter understands best," said Grandpa.

Mum looked round at everybody. Three soldiers knew he had to go. Dad knew he had to go. The doctor said he should go. Mum herself had only just changed her mind. The only one on her side was Grandpa, Kirsty thought. And Kirsty herself.

"He wants to stay," said Mum.

"Just take him," said Dad.

"No," said Mum, very loudly.

"Don't touch me," said Grandpa. "This isn't Siberia."

"Next best thing," said one of the soldiers. "Well, he seems to know what he wants, so we'd better leave him. Fold up the stretcher and we'll be off."

"Flying tractor," said Grandpa.

"Hush," said Mum. "They'll think you're foolish."

"He is," said Dad. "And not the only one." And he went off downstairs in front of the Army.

"He's right," said Mum, when the room was quiet again, and there was only the faint smell of helicopter left. "We're all daft. Maybe they should have taken you and me, Kirsty, and put us where we can do no harm."

"Happen," said Grandpa. "Now I've had plenty of company for the day."

"We'll be off," said Mum. "We know where you are. We'll watch it fly away."

Mum dug under the bed for Thingy, Kirsty picked up her bag, and they went out of the room.

"I'd better unpack," said Kirsty. "Stuff for Granny's."

"Yes," said Mum. "You'll not get there for a while."

The helicopter had whirled away the snow round it when it landed. There was a little left to billow about when it sped up its rotor and lifted off. It left that behind it and went clucking off into the sky, down the dale. Its shadow climbed the Brough and rippled up on to the top. The noise grew less, and then grew more.

149

"Coming back," said Kirsty. But it was Dad on the tractor, coming back from watching for himself.

"Well, that was useless," he said, angry with Mum, and with Grandpa. "What do you know better than the doctor?"

"I know by instinct," said Mum. "When all these machines and things get out of the way. Doctor listening with his boxes and stuff like that, just wanting to get a pill in him. It's what's natural that counts. That wants taking into account. If my Dad wants to stop in bed that's his affair, and mine, since I have to look after him."

"Aye, and I have all to do outside," said Dad.

"And so you would if they took him away," said Mum.

Dad had nothing to say to that, because it was true. But he was cross at everything going the other way from the plan, not really concerned with exact ideas.

"I'll be foddering," he said. "Late as it is."

"Cold out here," said Mum. "I'll make that tea."

"Not for me," said Dad. "No time."

Kirsty thought, if I started now I could get to Granny's before dark. But she knew she would not start now. She knew it was the wrong day. Today Mum needed her, to drink cups of tea with. And Grandpa needed a visitor, even if he didn't want one.

150

5

"All the things I haven't done today," said Mum. "There's been no time. And now there's the dinner to put on, and look at that mad clock on the wall. The electric must have been off for hours in the night." But when she looked at other clocks and watches, and could work out which were still going, it seemed that the electric clock hadn't stopped and the time was still only ten o'clock. "It doesn't make it any better," she said. "It's just more to do and all the energy's gone."

Mum had plenty to do, and used some of the time to have a cup of coffee. Kirsty had nothing to do, and filled up some of the time by having coffee with her — just enough in the milk to make the sugar taste.

Granny telephoned. She had seen the helicopter go over her house. She wanted to know whether Grandpa had got away safely. Mum finished her coffee at the telephone, and seemed to be set on using the rest of the whole day talking. Kirsty was not meant to understand most of the talk, and she didn't. She left the kitchen and went up to see Grandpa and look after his fire.

"Soon dealt with them," he said. "Off they went. They don't give you a chance, that's what."

Kirsty poked up the fire. It was going well. The room was warm, except at the ankles, where there was a draught. The fire pulled air into itself and got it from the floor.

"They're mad at each other," said Kirsty.

"Your Dad," said Grandpa, "always starts with the answer. He never gets at the question."

"My feet are getting cold," said Kirsty.

Grandpa's room had a couch in it as well as his bed and wardrobe and tallboy. Kirsty tried to shift the couch to the fire from its place beside the door, but it had sunk into the lino and its casters would not come out of the pits they had made. Grandpa got out of bed, quite easily, and lifted the end of the couch and helped Kirsty push it up to the fire.

"Are you all right?" she said. "You said you were dying. You can't move things about if you're dying."

"That's all right," said Grandpa. "It won't kill me. I'll die just the same."

Kirsty put her feet up on the couch. It was longer than her bed. It was like being a baby and lying in the bath in front of the fire. "You're a pretend," she said. She thought that would account for everything.

"No," said Grandpa. "It came on me this morning. I'll just die."

"Mum says you've done it before," said Kirsty. "She says it's just a mood."

"That's it," said Grandpa. "Being alive is another. If she knows a mood, then so do I. It's like butter. Sometimes it will come, and sometimes it won't."

"There's always butter," said Kirsty. "You just go to the shop and get it. It always comes."

"In the old days," said Grandpa, "when I was a lad, we made our own, and it wouldn't always come. You had to twine and twine on the handle until the cream made into butter, and there were plenty of days it wouldn't come so soon. Even butter can get in a mood."

Downstairs Mum was off the telephone for a time. Then it rang again, and she was on it for a little longer. Then she came upstairs.

"Well," she said, "I didn't know how to answer. That was the doctor with a thing or two on his mind, saying he won't stir for us again. But I've had that with him before, and been right." Mum enjoyed a fight with the doctor, or the milk people, or the council, and she always felt she had won. "You two look right comfortable," she said. "First-rate luxury up here. How are you, Dad?"

"Getting on with it," said Grandpa. "It takes a time. Take no notice of me. I'll get there alone."

"It's doing you good, whatever it is," said Mum. "You got chilled before, but you're right enough now. I remember being next door when you were this way once, and I was a little girl like Kirsty, and you were telling me of old days. They seemed long ago then, but they don't seem so far off now, not even twice as long as I can remember."

"It was a good while ago," said Grandpa. "Is it a good while till dinner, now? I'd just tell you about coming here, but you'd think I was wankly in my wits."

"Well, add it up with some other things, and you might be," said Mum.

"I was there," said Grandpa. "I know they never thought a word of it here, but I was there. It's how I got here. I was at Stony Ray."

Kirsty had a picture of Stony Ray in her mind, from summer time. A heap of stones, piled up a thousand years ago, two thousand years before, and some treasure under it, and hollow places where huge spiders had made great trembling webs they stood in the middle of and shook. At the top of the pile of stones was a column of stone standing like a finger. Then she had a picture of it in the snow, as it was today. Grandpa was talking about it in the snow, she knew.

"How did you get there?" she said, because she knew he had been lost, but Stony Ray wasn't far enough off to get lost. You would just walk down by the wall at the end of the Mire and come along the next wall over to the road, and that brought you to the farm.

"I didn't get there from here," said Grandpa. "Or I would have known the way."

"Nobody knows where he came from," said Mum.

"I began again there," said Grandpa. "I know I was a long time on the tops before I got to this pillar in the snow,

153

and that was the first time I got to the dying mood; or maybe the first time I was in it."

"But you never," said Kirsty.

"Saved up for later," said Grandpa. "But I was on with Stony Ray, up there like a signpost pointing no-ways, nothing to tell me where to go, and if it was, then black night and I couldn't read it. Or near black night, the ending of the day, and nowhere told for me to go, so I stood against this thing, in a bit of bield – shelter – and I stood, and I was just a bit of a lad, and clathery with cold and clemmed with hunger. Maybe I did more than part die out there then. I'll stop now, because you never believed it yet, any of you."

Kirsty said she had never heard it. But she knew what it was, because he had said before that Stony Ray had brought him here. Saying that it had happened was not the same as telling the story. Anyway, you dream, out in the snow under a wall. Did Boogie?

"That Stony Ray got behind me and pushed me away down to the farm yard," he said. "Through a gateway and in under a wall. That pillar of stone shifted off itself and got against my back and brought me here, and your great grandfather found me and brought me in. Being there, that's how I never got warm since."

"I've potatoes to do," said Mum. She had really been thinking about that. "Where did you come from before that?"

"I've forgotten by now," said Grandpa. "And I'll forget where I got to, and all, any time now."

"Real mystery man," said Mum unkindly in the door-way. "Oh, never mind, you won't say, will you?" but she said the last bit quite kindly.

"Perhaps you escaped," said Kirsty. "I'll go and help Mum."

Downstairs Mum said, "Well, he must believe it, so it's true for him, but it couldn't happen."

At dinner time Kirsty went down the yard and found Dad. Easy to find, he was chopping wood and sawing boughs ready to chop. A belt from the tractor whirled the circular saw, and the shadow of the belt licked the snow. Sawdust heaped up like cake crumbs.

"Is she that way out yet?" said Dad, when the tractor was quiet. "Like twined? Maybe you and me will have to watch ourselves."

Kirsty thought about that a little, while Dad picked up an armful of wood. "I'm all right," she said. "I'm not on anyone's side. It's you that's at it, not her and me."

"Then I'll just have to dodge," said Dad. Kirsty went ahead and opened the door for him. "And how is he?" said Dad, in a great cheery voice in the doorway. "How is he?"

"Middling," said Mum, very quietly. Kirsty could understand what Grandpa had said—Dad's question had really been the answer to itself, because the great cheery voice meant: you have to tell me he is very well indeed. "Why do you bother asking?" Mum went on. "You wanted him off to hospital. Take him away, you said."

"He's done it before," said Dad. "Always doing it."

"Then he can stay home, same as he always does," said Mum. "You just wanted him off in a helicopter. Uncle Fred in a helicopter, just like a grand joke."

"If he's dying," said Dad. "And the doctor . . . Well, maybe I'll just wash my hands and have my dinner."

I don't think I want any, thought Kirsty. Not if they're on like this. I get smaller when they're like this.

6

They went on being like this. Sometimes it was with words.

"I want to be at the sink to drain the potatoes," said Mum. "There's a perfectly good bathroom upstairs if you want to wash." She hadn't even stuck a fork in the potatoes to see whether they were done, before draining them. "I didn't work all that time to put a bathroom in and still not be able to get to the sink," Mum went on. She had worked and got the money for the bathroom, so Dad left the sink and went upstairs.

Kirsty tried to think of something calm to say, because there is room between words. But she could only think of telling Dad he could use her pink soap in the shape of a duck, and that seemed to have nothing to do with anything.

Sometimes it was without words. Kirsty could feel them both being very cross when they sat down. Between them, along one side of the table, there was a gap that neither of them went into. On Kirsty's side there was she, and she tried to sit in a joining-together way, but still they stayed three separate people. There was no Grandpa opposite to balance it all out.

And the potatoes had bones in their middles.

Kirsty took Grandpa's dinner up to him. Potatoes and

gravy, one a bit raw, the other scorched. She poked up the fire, hit his pillows, and stood in the quiet room a moment. It was too quiet.

"You're uneasy," said Grandpa. "Fidget. Go down."

She went down. Dad was eating all his potatoes. Mum was leaving the centres of hers.

"That was a rough do," said Dad.

"You, say nothing," said Mum. "Neither you, Kirsty." And all the dishes bounced in the sink, and the pans clattered on the hob. The cats yawned and crept about, and no one chased them away as they thieved the remains. Dad thought of several things to say and didn't say them, one after the other. Kirsty tried to think of things to say, but nothing came. Mum rattled away at the stove and brought out an apple pie. There was no sugar in it. The custard had lumps.

In fact the whole meal, and the people having it, had lumps.

Dad got up, trod on Thingy. Thingy swore. Dad swore. They went out of the house together, and went across the yard chatting.

Granny has a peaceful but busy house, thought Kirsty. She goes on with things without a fuss.

Granny doesn't argue. Her old dog Patch is a friend.

I wish I was there.

She went up for Grandpa's plates.

"It was a good pie," he said. "We never had that when I was a little lad. We had porridge and blue milk. You could see through the milk, and near on see through the porridge. But it was always good food here."

"It must have been the workhouse," said Kirsty. "It was porridge there. They read us this book at school."

"No,' said Grandpa. "I was a stable-lad. And they had horses here when I came, not tractors. Nor flying tractors."

Kirsty thought about flying horses, and picked his plates up. "I think I'll go to Granny's," she said. "I can walk down easily. Then I can go to school and see people."

"I'll lie here," said Grandpa.

"You won't die," said Kirsty.

"I can't keep the mood up long enough," said Grandpa. "But I know I'm going to wish I had. But nothing's happened that way yet."

"Then I can safely leave you," said Kirsty. "Until the snow's gone."

I'll just go, she thought, taking the plates down the stairs and into the kitchen. I'll just go and I'll ring up when I get there. It doesn't take long to get there, just over past the Mire and down the moor.

Mum was in the back room with some coffee, a cigarette, a fire, and a book. The cats were in the kitchen doing the washing up their way. The kitchen was an ugly tip.

Before I go, thought Kirsty. Before I go I'll put it straight. And she began to move plates about.

"Leave it," said Mum. "I'll do it when I'm ready."

Kirsty put the plates down. People don't like to be helped, she thought, sending the thought into Clara's mind through an eye that looked at her. Clara could look after herself, and didn't want help either. Cats don't need anything.

Kirsty looked at Mum. It was possible to read Mum's mind. She was not going to let Kirsty go to Granny's in the snow.

I'll ring up when I get there. It won't be long, if I don't go in the Mire. And I know about that. The weather is still sunny. I'll be all right to go. I would let my little girl go if I wasn't in a bad temper. I'm in a good temper, so she can go.

She went upstairs for her bag. She picked it up, then put it on her bed. It might have been all right in the helicopter, cabin baggage; it would have been all right in the ambulance; it could have been all right if she had been taking a sort of backstep, like two on a bicycle, on the doctor's skis. But it was not all right to carry all the way through the snow.

She took out what she had to have, just two things from them all, the whale with pyjamas in, and the spider. She decided that pink panther must stay and watch the rest, and that Chang could come instead. Chang and Patch understood each other, and no one here would miss him, because he was able to stay here as well as go with her. His mind worked that way.

The middle of the folded whale went in her pocket, with head and tail hanging out. Spider had several legs tied in a knot and went round her neck. He could hang down or sit up behind her head, whichever he preferred.

Mum went on reading downstairs. Kirsty put on her boots, picked up Chang, who was licking his feet, and went out.

Chang asked not to be put down in that snow. Mum called out something. "See you," said Kirsty. Chang put his arms round her neck and purred. Thingy came out of the door after them, and began to follow.

Kirsty went round the corner of the house. There was a wind. She had forgotten the wind. It was lifting the snow from the fields again, filling ruts and overblowing them, and making the ground indistinct. Kirsty turned to look at Thingy. He was walking along after her but getting visible and invisible in turn. It was a Changlike thing to do. Chang stayed visible and warm.

Away from the house the wind seemed to spread out and not be quite so pushy. Kirsty followed up a tractor track, where many people had walked. This was the way the tractor had gone to mark out the landing place, and the way the army had come and gone. The way wasn't just where Kirsty wanted to go, but she did not like to leave it.

I'm looking to see what it's like, she told Chang, putting her head to his and not saying the words.

She went on. Flying snow settled on the whale, round her middle but no higher. Chang dug in his claws and said he would not get down. Down under the snow Thingy said this was far enough.

They reached the circle the tractor had made. The ruts went across it, and so did the footprints. And then, at the middle, where the helicopter had landed, the prints stopped.

Kirsty looked round to see which way to go. She wanted to go across to the Brough, skirting the Mire, and go that way. Following the footprints had brought her a little out of her way. Now she looked for something else to walk towards.

There was nothing. Overhead the sky was bright and blue, and the sun was in it. There was no cloud in it. The cloud seemed to be on the ground, and from it. The wind had lifted so much snow now that nothing near or far could be seen. The Brough had gone into its whiteness, the farm had been swallowed. Stony Ray had melted. And it was hard to look anywhere, because the wind seemed to come from all directions and eat the sight from her eyes.

The sun itself went out. Like Grandpa under the sheet it was no longer to be seen. The light went, and all the shadows went with it. Nowhere stood all round Kirsty and the cats. But still, overhead, was the blue sky. So this whiteness was drifting snow, not falling snow.

Kirsty looked down for footprints. It might be best to go home, and the footprints would lead her there.

She could not see them. She could see above herself the sky, but down below nothing could be seen but a sort of white without light. At her shoulder she could see an outline of Chang, and that was all. At her feet she felt Thingy come close against her and call.

And a call from somewhere else too.

7

"I am not lost," she said to Chang. "They don't need to come for me." But Chang was not listening to her. He had heard the call as well, and had turned his head and moved his ears to hear it better, and where it came from. What Kirsty had heard might have come from anywhere.

Chang heard it again.

If I was at home, thought Kirsty. If I was at home as well, like Chang, sitting in the kitchen, until I got to Granny's. Because I am not lost.

I am not lost. I know where I am. I don't know where I am is that's all. I am where the helicopter landed. I could see it from the house, so I could see the house from here. But all that has gone away. I am in the middle of being in two places at once, with Chang.

The two places she thought of being in were Granny's kitchen and her own kitchen, but she was somewhere between, and they were calling her.

Lost is when you don't know where Here is. It is something to do with Here, not something to do with yourself.

I'm not lost. This place doesn't know where it is.

Then there was a sort of lowering of the whiteness, and she could see. There was only one thing to be seen, one thing not white, one thing not shapeless.

161

Not far off she saw the pillar on Stony Ray, standing and black. It was the only thing there was. She knew she was between Stony Ray and the house, nowhere near the Mire, the thing she must keep away from.

She wiped away some wetness from her face. Some of it was tears from her snow-stung eyes. Some of it was tears that had come on their own. She had to shift Chang about a bit to get her hand to her cheeks.

Why did Chang think the call had come from up there? It should have come from the house. She looked back, and snow went down her neck. There was no house down there.

She walked towards Stony Ray. Thingy, under her feet, walked with her. Spider hung heavy, like Chang. She knocked a cap of snow from its head. The whale was full of snow.

Granny will dry my pyjamas, she thought.

The black pillar stayed in sight. It looked lifelike and watchful. I am glad I found it, she thought, with Boogie in her mind as well, Boogie not far from the kitchen door that stayed shut all night, snow on his fur.

Stony Ray. The same name as the farm, the same thing in fact, because even at Stony Ray she would not have come very far.

Mum would still be by the fire, reading. Grandpa in bed by his fire, not doing anything but feeling better. And Dad probably foddering sheep. He must have called. But it was not his voice she had heard.

But it was fixed in her mind that Mum was by the fire, so she could not have called.

Chang got down into the snow. He landed on top of it and then sank in, which he was not expecting. He climbed up Kirsty and stood on her shoulder. He tried to get where he was before, and Kirsty tried to get him there, but every thing had moved and he couldn't settle.

There was a lifting of the blinding snow up into the line of sight again. Kirsty stood still, and wondered what she was standing with. Chang had come up again with cold feet, and she had the same thing, cold toes, and a pack of snow in her boot above the heel. The cold grew up her leg.

162

The wind dropped the snow again, and she saw Stony Ray again. It was not quite where she had expected, but over to one side, and still quite clear.

The wind moved me, she thought. Even if I stand still the wind moves me.

She changed direction a little. She was sure she changed direction. The feeling was not a part of being lost. She knew she had not moved on the ground. The snow must be sliding on itself.

Her feet came along with her, cold and not belonging. You can get frost-bite in the mind, she thought.

Chang became very awkward, walking round and round her face, and Thingy, at her feet, walked round the other way.

"Give up, both of you," said Kirsty aloud, stamping her feet gently so that she didn't tread on Thingy, and swimming her hands in front of her and knocking Chang off.

This time he stayed down, and even ran ahead a little, but that was because he was cross. He came back, and Kirsty would not let him get up again.

He turned to walk along his own footprints. Cats leave a single left foot mark and a single right one, neatly stitched over the snow. Chang tried to follow where he had been, but got a right foot in a left footmark, and began to get his legs crossed.

Kirsty thought that was very funny, and laughed at him, which made her feel warmer all over, and made Chang cross again. He sat down in the snow with his back to her and licked one of his feet.

"You can come up again," said Kirsty, and was going to pick him up. This time she had stopped with Stony Ray in sight. She knew exactly where it was. She had not moved from where she stood. She could prove it to herself by her own footprints and Chang's.

But Stony Ray had moved. It had gone quite a long way across to the right.

I haven't moved, she thought. I haven't turned. The pillar on Stony Ray has moved. And a new sort of cold came over her and down her back.

163

And then it became worse. She looked. The two cats looked. And the black pillar came towards her.

Stony Ray was moving. It was walking towards her.

The pillar was no longer black. She knew it had never been black, because it was made of grey stone, but it had stood black against the snow. Now it was grey, and walked grey against the snow.

It had a face. At the top where a face should be. A face looking at her, face-colour against the grey.

Kirsty could think of nothing but treasure. There was treasure under Stony Ray, and a fairy would lead you to it. But a fairy was something different, not a grey stone pillar that had come alive and grown a face.

Kirsty felt comfort from only one thing. She knew she could not speak, because her throat had gone dry; and she knew as well that you *must* not speak to anything guiding you to treasure.

That's what it is, she told herself. It will show me, that's all. It doesn't do anything.

The pillar came quite close. It came up to her. The cats went a little way off.

She thought of another thing. Chang would know about it. People can appear when they are not really there, a sort of a ghost, called a waff. This was a fairy or a waff.

The pillar, or the fairy, or the waff, spoke.

"This is bad weather," it said. "You must be Kirsty."

Kirsty opened her mouth and closed it. She was wanting to reply and couldn't, and could reply and didn't want to. She had said nothing.

The fairy went on. "I wondered who would be out in this weather, but you aren't far from home, are you?"

Kirsty thought this was worse than anything she had expected. This wasn't a piece of wandering stone, which would be strange, but seemed to have happened before. This wasn't a fairy to lead her to anything. This wasn't a waff, because a waff can't speak.

This was a witch.

Kirsty had never thought about moving stones, so she had no extra thoughts about them. She had wondered about fairies, particularly when she was younger. She had

164

heard about waffs, and hoped never to meet one. All these things she could in some way believe.

But she knew there were no witches outside the stories. But here was one, in front of her, looking at her, speaking to her. And now it was smiling. Here was something Kirsty did not believe in, clear in front of her eyes.

"You won't know me," it said. "So I won't bother saying my name. But we'd better go back to the house and get warm."

That proved it to Kirsty. She had wondered a bit, faced with a thing that didn't exist. But witches take you home with them, and that's the end. Home would not be a house, anyway, but a cave. Witches find you, take you away, and fatten you up and eat you.

She shook her head. She was not sure whether it moved. Her mind moved and said she would not go.

The witch put out its hand. This time Kirsty moved. She took a step back.

"It's not far," said the witch. "You're lost, aren't you?"

I won't speak to it, anyway, Kirsty thought. I won't go with it. I won't do anything.

"I'll carry you," said the witch, kindly.

But kindliness is dreadful in a witch. Kirsty turned and ran across the flying snow.

8

Kirsty did not run far. The snow decided the distance, and then it folded under her, tried to take a boot away, and dropped her down into itself. As she ran the cats frisked and scampered beside her like two dogs. Then, when she lay and floundered, they came and rubbed against her.

Kirsty was in a snow bank, in like an overblown sheep. The snow softened under her. She got up and tried to move further on, running, but only buried herself deeper in the soft stuff.

She could not go forwards, because that dug her into the hill. She turned round, and was in shelter. The snow was still being blown across her face, but not against the rest of her any more. And she had something behind her to be against. She leaned on it and it held her. She kicked her feet down and stood on firm ground. She felt warm out of the wind. She sat down. The two cats sat on her. Thingy mewed. He would rather be home. Chang licked Thingy's ear.

The witch had not followed. Kirsty watched her. The witch stood and looked. Kirsty looked back, and eased herself back into the snow bank. It creaked under her, and was a perfect chair, making itself exactly her shape.

But of course nothing was any better. The witch was still there. All she had done was put her hand back in her pocket, and it could come out at any time.

The wind still blew in Kirsty's ears. She wished she wore what the witch wore. It was a sort of head-mitten, she thought. But perhaps the rest of her was invisible, only a face showing. Kirsty pulled down her own glove and saw that she still had a wrist.

So one of them stood and the other sat, the wind blew the lifted snow past them, and nothing was any better. A corner of Kirsty's mind would keep thinking that she was doomed, that soon she would be taken and never hear of herself again. The rest of her was thinking that she was not far from home, or that if the witch went away, she was not far from Granny's house.

But which way was Granny's house? And which way was home? It was impossible to tell, surrounded by the shapeless whirls of snow in the air.

Then the witch began to be transformed. A light grew round her, brightness stood all over her, behind and in front, and Kirsty had to look away because of the dazzle.

The witch was smiling in all the radiance. Kirsty knew it was some sort of magic, and not at all real. It was not the same sort of thing as hoping that a fairy would lead the way to treasure. That would be real. This great light was not real, because it couldn't be, Kirsty thought. It was a magic act, and perhaps the snow would melt, but it would be an untrue enchantment.

The light began to spread. Its edge came towards Kirsty. She tried, with a sort of twitch, to get up, but her feet slid about and she stayed where she was. The light came upon her and walked over her and the cats.

It was sunlight, coming down from the sun above and getting to the ground again. On the way it had lit up the snow in the air like a spotlight. It was not witch work. It was weather work, and nothing to do with either of them.

The wind stopped. The snow rustled down from the air and lay still. The landscape settled on itself and the sun shone.

I ought to feel safe, Kirsty thought. In my igloo. But the witch was still there.

"I ought to take you home," said the witch. "Won't you come? You shouldn't stay out here."

Kirsty said nothing. She sat harder and the snow creaked.

All I have to do is sit here, Kirsty thought. She can't do anything. She isn't doing the weather. There isn't anything she can do. She felt that nothing more could come from the witch. She wanted to say "Go away" but that would break the rule of silence she had given herself.

She looked to see where she was. She was well up above where the helicopter had been, close by the wall going up to Stony Ray. The snow she was in was lying deep because it was against the wall. But she looked that way for only a moment, since it meant taking her eyes from the witch. Stony Ray stood there with its pillar, and more mounds of snow.

She put a hand through the snow behind her and touched the stone wall. It was a real thing, always there, part of the farmland, not like the snow or the witch.

Away down the hill the farm itself began to show. The wind had blown there for longer. First the trees showed, draped again with snow, and then the smoke of a chimney, and then the chimneys themselves, the roof, the walls, and the ground. Between Kirsty and the farm the place where the helicopter had landed was wiped clean of all marks, either blown away or covered.

"You don't know who I am," said the witch.

Kirsty thought, I do so. But she did not mind exactly who among witches this one was. A witch was bad enough, and nothing could be worse.

But it was. The witch said something that made matters even more unreal.

"I'm your Granny," it said.

Kirsty knew that was completely wrong. She was not the person that she just might have been, Grandpa's wife. Kirsty could remember her, from a long time ago, Grandma. Grandma had been short and Mum said fat but Grandma said plump, and Kirsty would have known her or her waff, the same as she would know Chang from any other Siamese cat, or Princess Marina from any other Jersey cow. And the witch was not Granny. No one has to explain how voices and the things you say are different. This was neither Grandma, nor Granny, with Patch and warm kitchen and walking stick.

It only showed how extremely stupid witches are. I don't have to worry about you, thought Kirsty. But it wasn't quite true. Perhaps you have to worry more about a stupid witch, who might be stupid because she was mad.

Granny would have worn sunglasses. Grandma wouldn't. She would have wrinkled up her eyes. Granny would have spoken to the cats.

"You should come with me," said the witch. "Now you know who I am."

Kirsty closed her eyes, put her head down on her knees over the cats, wrapped her arms round them and her head, and sat still and waited to be covered over with snow.

She waited. She heard the snow sparkling under the sun.

"We shall have to come for you," said the witch. Kirsty kept her eyes closed. She waited helplessly to be carried away. There was nothing more she could do. Perhaps she was not herself any more: if she was another person then it might be her Granny.

She waited a long time. Snow began to fall on her, new soft snow. The sun went away. She looked up.

The witch had gone.

Flakes of snow, not the hard lifted particles, blew across the ground, white against a grey background. Kirsty stood up and looked round her. She saw the pillar on Stony Ray and saw that it was not the witch again. She looked all round, and could not see far. The matted flakes were coming down too thick and fast, but when they touched the old snow they stayed low, while sliding along.

Kirsty had two cats on her shoulders. She stood and wondered how to manage them. Thingy did his best for her, she thought. He jumped down and ran off. She did not need to worry about him. He was young and strong, not like Boogie. She thought he might have gone home. Chang statyed where he was. He quite often expected to be carried even in good weather.

I'll start where I know, thought Kirsty, She came out from the snow bank and walked up the hill, and then went

169

into the snow again and stood right up against the pillar of Stony Ray.

It was deep in snow, so that her legs were not in the wind. It was wide enough to shelter the rest of her a little.

The wrong thing was that Stony Ray was not on the route from the farm to Granny's house. Between her and Granny there was now the Mire. The Mire drowned sheep. They would walk on it and go further and further, and then the ground was not ground but bog, and that was death to the sheep. It would be the same for a girl.

It might be the same for a witch. It's a bit equal, she thought, for witches and for me. I couldn't send Chang ahead because he is a valuable cat. Besides, he might be the imaginary half of him weighing nothing and the rest by the fire so it wouldn't prove. But just now I have got the heavy half.

I expect I could find the way across. I would rather find the way across than meet the witch again. She thought that, and knew there was something wrong with it. She wondered for a little while why she wanted to cross the Mire.

I feel a bit dreamy, she thought. And a bit cold.

Then Thingy came back to her and sat a little way off. He had long ears now, with black tips to them. He licked his foot.

9

Kirsty had had all the feelings there were already. She had felt frightened, angry, scornful, alarmed, desperate, and even dead. There was only one thing left for Thingy when he came back with long ears. She felt horrified.

She knew the whole world had gone wrong. Thingy should not change like that. In some ways she thought it was careless of him, and in some ways she knew it was not his fault, and that he might not even like it. But there he was, licking his foot still, with the long ears bent over his head.

She felt ashamed of hating him for being different. whether it was his fault or not didn't matter.

Perhaps I am changing too, she thought. Perhaps I wouldn't know if I had, or how I had. But my boots look sensible, and my gloves have hands in them. Chang is the same, and much too heavy, and my ears have not altered. I would feel the snow on them if they had.

Then her mind grew sensible. She saw that the thing with long ears was not Thingy. It was the same colour but without the patterns, and it had been hard to see that in the grey light, so she had made a mistake.

Long ears was a hare, the brown hare of the moorlands. She knew his track across snow. She had once thought each set of prints from the four feet was a single footmark from a tiptoe bird like an ostrich.

171

The hare stopped licking its printing foot and crouched. It might be looking. It might not.

That was all right for a time. Kirsty wanted to go to it and stroke it, to bring into the family with the cats. But she found she knew something else, and wished she did not.

Witches take the form of hares. How can I know such things? she said to herself. Why am I stupid enough to know and remember? The hare sat, and perhaps it watched and perhaps it did not.

If I had stroked it, she thought. Then it would have had me; then I should have been in its power. What went on in its mind? It was the witch mind in the head, and those ears were only a different sort of head-mitten to keep its schemes warm.

And Chang. What was Chang thinking, inside his head? Kirsty began to lower the arm that held him, slow, slow. His back legs began to go down her coat. His front claws clung and went through to her shoulder. She hung her arm down and there was nothing to hold him. He looked round behind him and dropped down to the snow.

Chase it away, Kirsty thought, sending him the message with all her mind. Chang looked at the snow, looked at the hare, walked across to it, and sat down face to face, and neither of them moved more than their noses.

It was a great help to be without Chang's weight. But it was a worry to see him enchanted so easily. She thought he had not tried.

There was a change in the weather now. The snow stopped blowing straight across and began to swirl gustily. At the same time there was more light overhead. She looked up and saw that there was something like an extra white sun high over her head, whirling and standing and sending light down so that she stood in it. It reminded her of the white light that once came from the witch before.

Snow was being sucked away from round her, lifted, and taken up. She saw the wind buffet Chang and the hare. They stared at each other, Chang with his forward-looking eyes, and the hare with its side-looking ones. Chang put his head forward and licked the hare on the nose. The hare grunted and hit him with one front foot and then the other, and settled down again.

Out from nowhere came another hare. It seemed to Kirsty to be the best thing she had seen all day. If there are two hares, she thought, then neither of them is a witch. The second one came and sat by the first. Chang altered his position so that he could watch both.

Then Thingy, the real Thingy, came back and chirruped at her, and sat down beside Chang, and four animals watched each other, and Kirsty watched them.

Stony Ray pressed against her. Snow had filled in behind her and she moved forwards. Snow had built up against Chang and the first hare, and they got up together. All four moved a little towards Kirsty, out of the deepening bank that had come against them.

There was more movement out in the snow. Another hare came close and stood, black ears hazy but distinct against the falling snow and in it.

All the animals moved away from her now, five of them gathered together in the calmest place of the turning flakes. They were no longer sitting down, but standing together, and it seemed that they were herded together by the wind, enclosed in a still part of the storm.

Kirsty was in the strong part of it. They know better than I do, she thought. They understand where to go. She went to them. The hares scattered for a time and then came back to where she was. She knew she had come to the right place, because in it the wind was least, or even nothing. And over her head there was a pillar of light that looked like a white sun from below.

Another hare circled the group, and was herded in by the dog of weather. They all came close against Kirsty's feet.

Then a black thing dropped against her feet. A big black bird stood there rustling an umbrella closed — its wings. It opened its mouth and said a word or sound, and steam stood in the air for a moment.

A raven, down in the eye of the blizzard. And a little way off, too shy to come right in, there was another one.

And I've nothing to feed them on, Kirsty thought. But she found in one coat pocket a calf-feeding pellet from

Princess Marina's breakfast one day. She dropped it down, and no one saw it. The animals had not come for food.

The wind tried to throw her over, and she had to move on. It was difficult not to tread on the animals now. They trod on her, she thought. She could tell there was weight on her feet sometimes, but they were cold enough not to be able to tell exactly what was happening. They were able to walk, though.

She could smell the raven. It smelt of warm dust. She pulled up Spider and smelt him. He smelt of house, under his hat of snow.

She looked round. Stony Ray had altered. It was just behind her still, but it was not so high. It looked now more like a steep-faced mound, and she could see it crawling forwards as the snow came towards her and fell down the steep face, and the wind lifted over her head. Stony Ray was sheltering them and moving with them. The snow went up and caught the light higher up and shone it down on them all.

So they moved slowly. Kirsty did not know where they were moving, but perhaps that did not matter. In one way it did not matter, because it was the only thing to do. If she stood still she would be buried, and the animals would go on without her. Hares and cats and ravens must know what they were doing; they have more sense of that kind than humans. Kirsty considered that she knew quite a lot, mostly about witches, but hadn't any sense like those of animals. She did not know about safety and keeping alive. She did not know whether she was keeping alive now. She thought the animals knew, and followed them. Besides, there was nothing else to do.

She followed them for ever. It must be a day and a night, she thought. It must have gone dark except for the light up there, and then come light again. I have been out here so long. But it is not seven years, because I did not speak to fairies or witches, only to Chang and Thingy.

Then she wondered whether the animals knew safety. They might be in the power of the witch, who was drawing them all down to her home. Drawing all living things to her, for the sake of Kirsty. Asking had not been enough,

174

pretending to be Granny had not succeeded. Now she had had to pull in other ways.

The witch was succeeding, Kirsty thought. She has got me going to her, and I have to go. I do not know what I shall do when I get there, but I am going to sit by her fire and I am going to pretend it is our kitchen or Granny's, and perhaps the witch will go away. I wish I knew magic. I would undo it all to summer and the hares could run about free, and I could go down to Granny's and back in the afternoon.

Because I don't like it here now. And she found that she was crying and sad, and went quite a long way crying and being sad. It had nothing to do with witches, or being out in the snow. She knew about those. She had a long cry, and felt better after it, but very uncomfortable because her face hurt, as it always does after a long cry, and hurt worse for being cold. And she had to wipe her nose with snow because there was no way of getting her handkerchief out.

After that she walked on better, and they were all moving faster, especially the wind, and that was whizzing the snow round them.

Then, all at once, the light went out. The wind went away. Nothing moved. There was darkness. It was probably the end of the world.

10

The sudden stop of everything made a silence that filled Kirsty's head with a sort of solid nothing. She was deafened with it. In a little while she found that the quiet was coming from outside. She heard her ears click when she swallowed. Then she could hear that there were other sounds.

The creatures at her feet moved. At first a little, and then snow moved against her again, and all at once the hares scattered and ran away. She heard them and saw them go, and it seemed as if they were flying, because they went up into the air.

On either side of her were huge banks of snow, and the hares had run up them and gone. She knew their prance and walk. Up one bank, but not with the hares, went Chang. And then there was a true flying. The raven unfurled its wings, spoke a raven word, and flew up past her face and away into the darkness.

Now there was silence. She was alone. She had not seen Thingy go, but he was not at her feet. He must have gone into the darkness ahead, where Kirsty could see nothing.

She looked round. She was in a bowl of snow. It had mounded up behind her and on either side. But ahead was the darkness, and she did not like to turn her back on it. Nor did she want to walk forwards into it.

The silence went on. Under the silence, but not breaking it, was the murmur of the wind. Stray flakes of snow still fell on her.

Then there was a sound. It was a clicking rattle. It was a sound she knew, small and continuous, not very far away to the front. But she did not know what it was. It was familiar but did not belong here, and it frightened her.

Then there was a light. It was a very small light, the size of a candle-flame. But a candle-flame gives light as well as being it. This little light only was light and did not give anything out.

It came and went, not flickering, as a flame would, but being there and then not being there, and coming again.

Somebody began singing.

It was no song that you would know; just someone singing to herself, comfortably, and coming nearer.

Kirsty decided that she was doing it herself. But she knew the singing was like the silence, coming from outside. And still the light twinkled.

I'm looking down on the sky, she thought. That's a star. But stars don't sing. I don't know what anything is today. I don't think I am here any more.

The rattling went on. The singing came closer.

Then she could see ahead. There was more light, but she could not tell where it came from. She saw the snow banks clearly now. She saw a doorway in front of her, and a door in it, and in the door there was a keyhole and the little twinkling light came through the keyhole. It came and went because Thingy was hanging on the loop of the sneck, rattling the latch, making the noise she heard. And the other side of the door was the singer, coming towards it.

She should have known the sound, and who had made it. It was Thingy's trick to climb on the loop and rattle. Dad called him a rattle-sneck. Chang had too much dignity to do that. He expected doors to be opened for him.

Of course, seeing what was there explained some things. It did not explain why they were there, or where she was, or who was singing.

Seeing took five seconds. No time to think what to

177

think or do what to do. Then it was too late. The door opened. It opened just as Kirsty knew what would open it, just as she knew she was doomed.

It was the witch that opened the door. She had her head-mitten off now, but still had her coat on, and she was in her kitchen with the fire lit.

Thingy fell off the door and walked in. He sat on the rug by the fire.

"Come in," said the witch. "You've been out there long enough. You'll be chilled through."

And Kirsty was so glad that for once today the thing she had expected was the one that came to pass, that she walked straight into the witch's kitchen. For once the thing she came across was no worse. She felt pleased, as well as being as doomed as ever. And there was nothing else to do. She had been caught.

She tramped in, blinking in the light. The witch had electric light. Kirsty stood in the middle of the floor and snow fell from her all round.

The door closed.

"Well, I am glad you came," said the witch. "I didn't know what to do."

Thingy started to wash, as if he was at home. It was Thingy: there were no long ears to him now. Kirsty stood, and her fingers began to ache.

"I was right worried," said the witch. Her head-mitten was on a chair, lying like a grey cat. At the windows there stood the white ghosts of snow looking in. "What'll she do, out in that?"

Then, click, she slid a bolt over on the door. "It wants fixing up tight," she said. "I think you'd better go out again through the other room, and tell them next door that their little lass is found." She led the way through into the back of the house, and Kirsty followed. She would be locked up, she knew. But the witch opened a door out into the snow again. "They're waiting to hear," she said.

11

The next door was a few paces away. Kirsty did what she was told and walked to it in the dark. The witch was at her door watching. More of them in the next house, thought Kirsty. She came to the door. She put her hand on the sneck, lifted the latch, and walked in. She knew her own kitchen door when she saw it.

What she thought did not have time to catch up what she did. She knew her own kitchen when she got into it. I'm doing all ordinary things, she thought, but in an extra different way, because I don't expect to be here, and I don't understand.

Mum was standing by the stove. Dad was at the foot of the stairs stepping into his boots. He had put on dry socks.

"There's a snowball got in," said Mum, looking at Kirsty.

Kirsty thought she would kneel down. Or the kneel-down thought it would happen. But it was a sort of dizziness beginning at the knees and coming up through her middle and into her head, so she found she was lying down quickly but that there was nothing in her clothes any more.

She did not manage to obey the witch. She forgot to give the message.

But Mum was there, and warm fingers were taking her

coat off, and a big hand was holding a knee and taking off her boots, because Dad was helping. And Clara came to look in her eye.

"I was just off to look for you," said Dad. He had her up in his arms. "Betty came in and told us you were off in the snow somewhere."

"Betty?" said Kirsty, but the first time she spoke her tongue did not belong. It had not been used in a long time. "Betty?" she said.

"You just lie here," said Dad, putting her down by the fire in Grandpa's room, on the couch.

He and Mum had changed ends on her. He was pulling her sleeves long to get a wet jumper off. She was pulling off snow-matted socks. In a few minutes Kirsty was wrapped up in blankets, watching the fire.

"There'll be tea in the pot," said Dad. "I'll get it."

Kirsty lay there for a little longer. The wind called outside. The fire cracked. Chang and Hubert came up to sit by it. Hubert came and sat on her.

"Out in the dark," said Mum. "A daft trick. Do you feel better now?"

"Yes," said Kirsty. "Was that Betty? But she said ..." and then she stopped remembering about who was Granny, and what that meant.

"She wondered what you'd taken her for," said Mum. "But you don't know her, so it's no wonder. There's two of you daft, out there this weather. There's three of you daft altogether, if you ask me. Him there, he's worst, your Grandpa. There's only me and Dad and some sane cats left."

"I don't know how to manage some things," said Grandpa. He was sitting up in bed now, looking perfectly well, and a bit found out but not ashamed of it.

"Betty's his girl friend," said Mum. "As if I didn't know. We thought she was playing you up, didn't we, Kirsty?"

"She never would," said Grandpa.

"No," said Mum. "These socks will never dry. They've got glaciers where some people have holes. You tell her, Grandpa."

"It's nothing much when it's got out," said Grandpa.

180

"But I didn't like to say. I just thought I'd get wed again, today like, go down after milking and get fixed up. But with me being just like a visitor here, like I told you, getting brought here by Stony Ray, but you think it's just a tale."

"I don't," said Kirsty. "I was up at Stony Ray and the wind blew, and it blew me and Stony Ray, down to the house."

Or did it? she wondered. Where did I get to?

"Did it?" said Grandpa. "Then I know it happened too. I thought I could be mad all these years, because I knew it happened but it couldn't. I couldn't believe. I left my work. I'd got in a bad way down at the stables, and I never got my work done that morning, I never saw to my horse, and I didn't want to get beaten. You have to see to your stock. I think I was on about it this morning, out of the same reason. So I ran away. And I always knew I would have died if it hadn't been for Stony Ray getting at the back of me and pushing me down here in the yard. So here I've stopped, like a visitor. Then I got a fancy for Betty, and it was to be today; but it isn't my house here or next door, and, well, I couldn't say anything. So I thought I'd best get in my bed and stay there a day or two and die proper, and get no more problems."

"Die proper," said Mum. "Daft proper. You'd only to say. There's that house empty beside us, wanting using, and you don't need to ask; you've only to say it's yours."

Dad began to come up the stairs with some tea.

"Betty's got more sense, like I said," said Mum. "Right plain sense, too. When he didn't land to get wed she came on here to roust him out. She met you on the way and she wanted to bring you back, but you wouldn't come."

"I thought she was a witch," said Kirsty. "I thought plenty of things about her. Too much plain sense – she thinks you know."

"Can I come in?" said the witch. "I brought your tea up, and a cup for Fred. Can I sit on your couch end?" She did, anyway. Kirsty pushed her feet against her. It would be convenient, having a Granny next door as well.

"Came in the door like a snowman," said Betty, witch, Granny-next-door.

Hope she stays a bit of a witch, thought Kirsty. She can borrow a cat if she needs it.

About the Author

WILLIAM MAYNE completed a first novel at the age of sixteen and decided that writing would be his career. Since his first work for children was published in 1953, Mayne has written over sixty books. His novels include *A Grass Rope*, for which he won the Carnegie Medal, *A Swarm in May*, *Earthfasts*, and most recently for Delacorte Press, *Drift*.

William Mayne lives in a small cottage in the Yorkshire dales.